W9-AAY-675

shine,

coconut moon

neesha meminger

MARGARET K. McELDERRY BOOKS
New York   London   Toronto   Sydney

MARGARET K. McELDERRY BOOKS

An imprint of Simon & Schuster Children's Publishing Division

1230 Avenue of the Americas, New York, New York 10020

This book is a work of fiction. Any references to historical events, real people, or real locales are used fictitiously. Other names, characters, places, and incidents are products of the author's imagination, and any resemblance to actual events or locales or persons, living or dead, is entirely coincidental.

Copyright © 2009 by Neesha Dosanjh Meminger

All rights reserved, including the right of reproduction in whole or in part in any form.

MARGARET K. McELDERRY BOOKS is a trademark of Simon & Schuster, Inc.

For information about special discounts for bulk purchases, please contact Simon & Schuster Special Sales at 1-866-506-1949 or business@simonandschuster.com.

The Simon & Schuster Speakers Bureau can bring authors to your live event. For more information or to book an event, contact the Simon & Schuster Speakers Bureau at 1-866-248-3049 or visit our website at www.simonspeakers.com.

Also available in a Margaret K. McElderry hardcover edition.

Book design by Debra Sfetsios

The text for this book is set in Minion Pro Regular.

Manufactured in the United States of America

First Margaret K. McElderry paperback edition June 2010

10 9 8 7 6 5 4 3 2 1

The Library of Congress has cataloged the hardcover edition as follows:

Meminger, Neesha.

Shine, coconut moon / Neesha Dosanjh Meminger. —1st ed.

p. cm.

Summary: In the days and weeks following the terrorist attacks on September 11, 2001, Samar, who is of Punjabi heritage but has been raised with no knowledge of her past by her single mother, wants to learn about her family's history and to get in touch with the grandparents her mother shuns.

[1. Family—Fiction. 2. Prejudices—Fiction. 3. East Indian Americans—Fiction.
4. Sikhs—Fiction. 5. High schools—Fiction. 6. Schools—Fiction.
7. September 11 Terrorist Attacks, 2001—Fiction.] I. Title.

PZ7.M5178 Sh 2009

[Fic]—dc22

2008009836

ISBN 978-1-4424-0305-5 (pbk)

ISBN 978-1-4391-5835-7 (eBook)

To Hollis, for working so hard to turn our possibilities into probabilities

Acknowledgments

A big, giant thank-you to Satya and Laini, for showing up just when I thought I had it all figured out and dragging me right back to square one—together, you've taught me how much I don't know and turned my life upside down (in the best possible way). A whole-heart thank-you to Hollis—all of this is because you're at my side. Special thanks, also, to Balbir, Jagdish, Manjit, and Daljeet Virk, for providing the raw material for all my stories.

An abundance of gratitude to the awesome Karen Wojtyla, for working her editorial magic; and to Sarah Payne for her warmth and promptness. Thank you also to the crew at McElderry Books for their polishing skills and attention to details, big and small.

To Steven Chudney, Nikki Hart and the Hart clan, the Rawlins clan, C. Lee McKenzie, Donna St. Cyr, and Julie Swanson for sharing their stories; Priya Raju and Dr. Jerry Ahluwalia for their invaluable assistance during my research into emergency room and medical procedures; the Barracudas in JWA, Verla Kay's Blue Board, the gals of SAWCC-BEG, SWONY, and the Debs for their unrelenting support and camaraderie; and all authors who have inspired me as well as those who continue to inspire me.

Finally and firstly, to the ancestors and the Great Spirit—the Grand Poobah of all authors.

Chapter 1

There is a man wearing a turban ringing our doorbell. I walk slowly up the driveway and stop a safe, short distance from him as he rings again.

"Yes?" I ask, cautiously. Is this guy a salesman? Lost, asking for directions? Strange, weirdo lunatic? We're not expecting anyone, as far as I know, and all of Mom's clients use the separate entrance to her basement office.

The man jerks around. "Samar . . . ?" he says, his eyes widening. He steps toward me.

Okay, strange, weirdo lunatic—who knows my name! I shift the bag I'm holding, with my brand-new pedicure kit in it, to my other hand and take a quick step back in the process. Because of the pounding in my ears, my voice comes out as a shrill squeak. "Who wants to know?"

He stops and puts his hands in his pockets, his smile fading. "You don't recognize me," he says. He looks down as if he's lost something.

I grip my shopping bag tighter and squint at him. *Recognize* him? What is he talking about? Why would I recognize him? I *know* that I don't know any turban-wearing, dark-bearded, and mustached men. There aren't any on our street, that's for sure.

Is that it? Maybe this guy *is* lost. But then, how does he know my *name*?

"Samar," he says, shifting his weight from one foot to the other. "I'm your Uncle Sandeep, your mother's younger brother. Do you remember me at all?"

My throat goes dry as I look into his face. The only uncle I have is in my mother's photo albums. An uncle I haven't seen since I was a baby—and no, I don't remember him at all. But this guy looks a lot like that uncle.

I swallow hard and shake my head. My voice comes out as a hoarse whisper. "I don't remember you."

He reaches into his pocket and I jump. He holds up a hand. "It's okay," he says, pulling out a wallet. He flips through some cards and holds one up for me to see; an ID card for a gym membership. Under the photo is his name, Sandeep Ahluwalia.

"No, I *recognize* you, from my mom's photos, but I don't *remember* you . . . from my childhood."

He clears his throat, color rising in his face. He steps forward with a hesitant smile and holds out his arms. When I don't make any move toward him, he drops one arm and extends the other. I falter, but then offer my hand, which he promptly engulfs with both of his and proceeds to pump enthusiastically.

"Samar, look how grown you are—I can hardly believe my eyes! You were only a baby when I saw you last."

Why are you here? I want to say, but I stand there mutely while my arm is all but wrenched off my body.

He finally lets go of my hand and steps back. He looks like he's trying not to sweep me up in his arms, so I scoot around him, leaving plenty of room between us, and leap up the porch steps to the front door. "Wait here," I say. "I'll go get Mom."

Mom usually sees clients on weekdays, but since some of them work and can't make it in during the week, she sets aside a few hours on Saturday mornings for them. Almost all of her clients are women who have "issues stemming from childhood."

I let the door slam behind me, drop my bag, and run downstairs to Mom's basement office. I'm about to pound on her door, right underneath the gold plaque with SHARANJIT AHLUWAHLIA, MSW engraved on it, when she flings it open.

"Sammy! Is everything all right? I just heard the door slam and then you running down the stairs."

"Mom, there's a guy upstairs claiming to be your long-lost brother."

She stops short. "There's a what?"

"Uncle Sandeep, the guy from the pictures in your album— at least that's who he says he is. He's standing upstairs. On our front steps. Right now."

"Impossible." Her face drains of its usual honey warmth. She turns slowly to walk up the stairs. I follow on her heels.

When we get to the door, we both peer through the small window in the kitchen. The man is still there, staring up at the faint traces of smoke left behind by a passing plane. Mom opens the door quickly and steps outside. I slip out just in time to miss having it smack me in the face.

"Yes?" she says, just a bit too loudly.

The man whirls around. "Sharan!" He takes a long stride toward her. His face is beaming and his eyes are shiny. Then he stops abruptly. I look at Mom's stricken face. If I had any doubts at all before, they disappear now: This guy is, without a doubt, her brother. She looks frozen solid. I move closer to her.

"Sharan . . . I'm sorry to come by out of the blue like this. . . ." He plunges his hands into his pockets.

"What do you want?" Mom asks firmly, sounding and looking more like the mom I know.

"Just to talk, Sharan. Nothing more," he says softly. "We let far too much nonsense get in the way. . . ."

"*We?*" Mom arches her eyebrows.

"Yes, *we*: me, and Ma and Papa."

Mom's shoulders inch down slowly from where they were, hunched up near her ears, as my pulse starts racing. My uncle is standing here. Live and in the flesh. A member of Mom's estranged and mysterious family.

"Why now?" she asks. "All these years you could have visited, called . . . something, *anything.*" Her voice cracks on the last word.

"You're right," he says, his voice husky. "But we're living in different times now, Sharan, and I want to be close to the ones I love. The world is in turmoil—war is raging. Anything could happen at any moment. So many people lost loved ones on what they thought was just another ordinary day. . . ." He trails off before looking up at her again. "Yes, it has been many years, and I know it may take just as many to make it right. But Sharan, let's just talk, at least? Then, if you want, you can kick me out and call me names and tell me never to come back. It'll be just like when we were kids." He gives her an uncertain grin.

That seems to crack through some of Mom's shield. She swallows, and the muscles around her mouth relax a bit more. "You never would get lost, even then."

This time he grins for real. Mom hesitates, then steps aside. But instead of walking past her to the door, he folds her in his arms in an embrace that is awkward and tender and warm all at once. I see Mom slowly untense until her arms go around his shoulders as well.

Since my dad left when I was about two, I don't think I've ever seen her hug a grown man. She tried dating a few times, but that never amounted to anything. Now she says she's got her work, her friends, and me—what else does she need? I could think of at least one or two other things, but I usually keep them to myself.

My heart races with possibility. This is a member of Mom's family! *My* family. The family that I've asked about a million times and never gotten any clear, direct answers, except that they were "miserable, critical, and controlling people."

When they part, there's a damp stain on Uncle Sandeep's shirt in the place that Mom's face was buried. He dabs at the inside corners of his eyes. Mom takes my hand as we walk up the steps.

Inside, she ushers her brother into a seat next to her at the kitchen table. "Would you like some tea?" I ask him. All of a sudden, I feel inexplicably shy. And a bit jittery, like I just drank several shots of espresso or something.

"Just water, please."

"Mom?" I ask, holding up a glass. She nods and bends down to scratch her ankle. The outline of her yin-yang tattoo peeks out on the back of her neck, half covered by her lime green sweater.

"Nice tattoo," Uncle Sandeep says.

She absently fingers the outline on the back of her neck. "I got it a few months after what's-his-name left." She still won't say my biological father's name out loud. All she will say is that he decided marriage with her was not what he wanted. And, since he was a son in an Indian family, his parents made it all her fault. Said she was too argumentative and out of control.

Which could very easily be true, though it would be hard to tell, given that Mom's parents were *super*-religious Sikhs when she was growing up—not letting her cut her hair, shave her legs, go out with her friends, and expecting her to marry someone *they* picked. She says that's the reason she bolted. Super-religious parents + major restrictions = unhappy Mom walking out the door forever.

Except now Uncle Sandeep just walked back in said door. All of a sudden, an unsettling thought flits across my mind: Does he think he's going to come back around and be some kind of "male authority figure" in my life? If so, he's got another think coming. I walk around to Mom's other side and sit down next to her with conviction.

He, in contrast, gets up, turns his chair backward, and sits with his knees on either side of the backrest, resting his chin on the top of it. "I like your place." He looks at me with a warm smile. "In some ways," he says, turning to Mom, "it feels like only a few days since I last saw you. You look exactly the same, Sharan, except for the gray hair." His eyes glint with mischief.

"And your paunch," Mom shoots back, winking at me.

Good one, Mom. I grin and relax a bit, wondering why Mom has been so uptight about her family. He seems okay, this guy . . . Uncle Sandeep.

He laughs. "Sharan, I've missed you."

"Your dialing finger doesn't *look* broken," Mom says, eyeing his hands.

He smirks. "Touché. When you got married, I was young and dumb, Sharan. I thought Ma and Papa were right, and that you were only making trouble to annoy them. I blamed you for ruining everything. Then I got married, and that started changing my perspective a little."

"I got the invitation to your wedding. I just couldn't attend, Sandeep." There's a hint of remorse in her voice. She sighs and runs a finger along the rim of her glass. "It was right after the whole thing with what's-his-name, and the entire family was there. I just couldn't face the stares, and the whispers and questions. I went through enough of that when I was a teenager."

He nods. "I didn't expect you to be there. Ma and Papa were hoping you'd show up anyway, for appearances' sake."

"Typical. That's all they ever cared about," Mom says. "I'm

sorry it didn't work out with Baljit. I heard from Jasleen Dhatt that you were getting divorced."

"The marriage had been deteriorating for some time, but neither of us wanted to admit it," he says, looking up at the ceiling. "We separated about two years ago, and the divorce was finalized six months ago. That's when I got the slightest taste of what you must've gone through with Ma and Papa during that whole mess—"

Mom glances at me. "And then you realized you missed your big sister," she concludes quickly.

"And then I realized how lonely it can be without family around." He pauses to give her a meaningful look as his eyes flit briefly over me. "I had it out many times with Ma and Papa over the last few years about my marriage, and I missed you terribly. I wanted so much to pick up the phone and talk to you, but I remembered how final you were—how angry—about everything when you cut us off."

He drops his chin to his chest for a moment before looking back up. "Ma and Papa are a pain, yes. No arguments there. But they're still Ma and Papa. And you're a bossy know-it-all, but only you know what life was like growing up with them. I miss conspiring against them with you, even though you made all the plans and I got caught implementing them."

Mom yields to a small smile. "Not *my* fault you were slow and clumsy, always rushing ahead without getting all the facts."

Steadily, the interaction between Mom and Uncle Sandeep becomes easy and fluid, as if only a few months have passed since they last saw each other, not fifteen years.

And when I really think about it, I can recall her talking to her friends about how much, above all else, she missed her brother. And the times she seemed most nostalgic were the rare moments when she shared a happy memory from her childhood that included Uncle Sandeep. At those times, the look on her face reminded me of the times I went for sleepovers at my best friend Molly's house and felt homesick.

"Samar." He turns his whole body to look at me. "Do you remember the little yellow Winnie the Pooh stars and moon blanket I gave you when you turned two?" It takes a moment to register exactly what he's saying, but when I do, my jaw drops.

That Winnie the Pooh blanket was the only thing that helped me fall asleep after my father left. I have faint, wispy memories of crying for my "yum-yum" and desperately searching for it. By the time I stopped using it, I was six and the thing was tattered, gray, and almost see-through. And it's still upstairs in my trunk.

"*You* gave me that?"

"Gosh, I'd forgotten all about that," Mom says, shaking her head slowly.

Up until this very moment, I had seen this man as a sort of fascinating but familiar stranger; a brief glimpse into Mom's— and my—mysterious past. Not someone who knew me before my yum-yum.

As Uncle Sandeep gets up to leave, I see the faint outlines of what once must have been a strong bond between Mom and Uncle Sandeep. It zings, sort of like an invisible current of shared pain, secrets, and loyalty. There's a kind of elation that I've never seen before in Mom's eyes. Something like hope.

Uncle Sandeep turns to me. "The real reason I wanted to come back into your lives," he says conspiratorially, "is so that I can bring Samar here up to speed on the details *you* have undoubtedly left out about your sordid past." He throws his head back and laughs an evil-villain, *mwa-ha-ha* laugh.

I perk up. "What details?"

"There *are* no details," Mom says quickly. "I keep no . . . very *little* . . . secret."

He winks at me and leans in close. "Did she ever tell you about her boyfriend Moose?"

"*Moose*, Mom?" I widen my eyes.

Mom glares at him. "I get the feeling I'm going to regret ever letting you back in the door, Sandeep." She gets up and walks him to the door.

Before Uncle Sandeep walked back into my life, I'd never cared that I was a Sikh. It really didn't have much impact on my life, especially since Mom is a hard-core atheist. But that was before 9/11.

The Saturday morning that Uncle Sandeep rang our doorbell had one of those endless, frozen blue skies hanging above it; the same kind of frozen blue sky that, just four days earlier, had borne silent witness to a burning Pentagon and two crumbling mighty towers in New York City. And the cause of all those lost lives was linked to another bearded, turbaned man halfway around the world. And my regular, sort of popular, happily assimilated Indian-American butt got rammed real hard into the cold seat of reality.

Chapter 2

In Linton, New Jersey, people have slowly started to get back into their daily routines, but everyone's still on edge. We're supposed to not let "them" win, by continuing with our lives like nothing happened. The president and other politicians urge everyone to go on shopping and doing business like normal, while television news, magazines, and newspapers showing images of the attacks over and over make that pretty much impossible.

Ads run every few minutes during my favorite TV shows, depicting smiling faces of every race and ethnicity, saying firmly, "*I'm* an American." And even though we're three hours away from New York City, all the buildings have beefed up security procedures; the announcements at school tell us to report any "suspicious packages" or "unattended backpacks"; and every time a car backfires, tensions rise like simmering water. And now there's the thing with anthrax. Whenever I walk by the office at school, I see the secretaries opening mail with rubber gloves on.

When I'm home, Mom makes me focus on other things, like

schoolwork, or she brings home some comedy and romance DVDs, or she encourages me to hang out with my best friend, Molly, and "go be a teenager."

Today I'm on my way to Molly's house. They're having a huge birthday celebration for Molly's great-aunt Maggie. I love and hate Molly's huge family gatherings. Love, because her family is awesome—they're a blast to be around, and warm and welcoming. Hate, because when I'm in the midst of all that laughter and familyness, I feel more alone than ever.

But since Molly is my best friend, and because she hates huge get-togethers, especially ones that involve her family, I *have* to be there. It's one of the clauses in the best-friend handbook.

When I get there, the place is already swarming with family. Someone grabs my hand and yanks me into the living room. Someone else hands me a red plastic cup with something that looks like cranberry juice sloshing over the edges. Mrs. MacFadden, Molly's mother, scurries over to take the cup from me. "Oh, heavens!" she says to the man who handed me the drink. "Jack, that punch is not for the kiddies!" She ushers me to another table. "Here, darlin'," she says, ladling something bubble-gum-smelling into a cup decorated in a Clifford the Big Red Dog theme. She pats the top of my head brightly and sashays away. I peer into the watery, powdery mixture, put the cup down, and head back to the other table.

Molly jumps in front of me out of nowhere. "Finally!" she says, grabbing my arm and steering me into the kitchen. "I've been waiting *forever*." She leans closer and whispers, "I have some 'fun' in a thermos over here. Just keep it on the DL—it smells like orange juice, so no one has to know a thing."

The kitchen is where the rest of the crew is. Everyone has plastic cups with some of Molly's "fun" juice. A couple of the cousins I've met before at MacFadden family events grin and do a mock toast as I walk in. Molly rummages around in the cupboard under the sink, then stealthily pours some of the juice into a bright orange cup. She quickly caps the thermos, shoves the cup into my hand, and slams the cupboard shut as her uncle Jack does a little two-step dance into the room.

"Hey there, young'uns!" he says boisterously. He eyes the opaque plastic cups containing our fun-juice and smirks. "Glad to see a group of youngsters concerned about their daily dose of vitamin C!"

Molly's cousin Peggy, whom I met a couple of Christmases ago, grins and holds up her cup. "Haven't you seen the commercials, Uncle Jack? Most teens don't get enough fruits and vegetables in their diets!" He lets out an explosive laugh and slaps his thigh as he heads back into the family room, where Great-Aunt Maggie sits.

Great-Aunt Maggie is seated in the center of the family room like a giant centerpiece around which a lot of the adult relatives sit, chat, and drink. The other centerpiece, getting a lot more attention than Great-Aunt Maggie—and even she can't seem to keep her eyes off it—is the giant new flat-screen TV that Molly's dad bought last week. It literally takes up half the wall in their big family room.

More and more people file in through the front door: women in dresses carrying casserole dishes covered with aluminum foil, huge Crock-Pots with stew, or boxes of desserts; men with shirts straining to make the full journey around their midriffs; drooling babies; screaming toddlers; bored-looking thirteen-year-olds; grandparents pinching cheeks and calling everyone by the wrong name . . .

For someone like me, who's used to cozy, two-person-and-maybe-a-couple-of-friends celebrations, Molly's family "events" are always a bit dizzying. Because this is Great-Aunt Maggie's ninety-second birthday, today is more like a family reunion than a birthday party. I can't believe how many people are able to squeeze into the MacFadden house.

"Let's go up to my room," Molly says, again grabbing my arm, this time steering me upstairs. "It's the only place we *might* be able to get some privacy."

On the way up to her room, we pass an eight-year-old drawing on the wall with what looks like a block of cheese. Molly shrugs and takes another sip from her cup.

Once in her room, Molly puts her drink on the dresser and flops onto her bed. "Aaarrghh! Help, this place is insane!" she says, laughing.

I feel a familiar pang slice through me, the same one I get every time I'm surrounded by Molly's enormous and loud family. I shove the feeling aside. "Looks like everyone's having fun," I say, shrugging.

If I had to describe it, I would say Molly's family is a painting in bright, vibrant colors, while my family—meaning me and Mom—is bland neutrals and beiges in a taupe frame. Molly's family is 100 percent, no question, without a doubt, Irish. They all know it, celebrate it whenever possible, and broadcast it with great pride.

She rolls onto her back and closes her eyes. For a few minutes we listen to the sounds from downstairs: shrieks and squeals of delight, sudden thunderclaps of laughter, people yelling over one another to be heard, clinking of glasses, cheers, and whistles.

"Anyway," she says, eyes flying open again, "have you figured out what you're going to get Mike for his birthday?"

I shake my head to clear the lonely feeling that had begun to roll in. "He said he wants a quiet night in, so I thought I'd spice it up a bit," I say, dipping a hand into my bag. I pull out the one-piece I bought—a royal blue, satin, Western-cowgirl type, with fringes over the underwire part of the bra and a thong back.

Two years ago, when we turned fifteen, Molly and I began collecting lacy, elegantly slutty undergear. We decided that was the year we would both lose our virginity, and lingerie seemed to be a good first step. I'm sure it had nothing to do with the fact that Bobbi Lewis and her minions were talking in gym class about how you can't explain what it's like to have sex— you just have to *do* it. Or with her casually glancing around the room, and saying with her nose in the air, "It makes you a *real* woman, not like most of the little girls running around at this school."

Since then we've been steadily building our arsenal of slinky underthings in preparation for the Real Deal—our first time. I'm pretty sure my Real Deal will be with Mike, but the time hasn't been right yet. Molly's main concern is finding the right guy. She's bored with Melville's offerings and is considering branching out to some of the neighboring schools.

The lingerie was Molly's idea, and going to the Center for Young People for a workshop on birth control was mine. My mom's pretty cool, but if I ever came home pregnant—first-born only daughter or not—she would *kill* me.

There's a faint knock on the door. "What d'you want?" Molly asks, without getting up.

A little girl's voice says, "Molly, do you want to have a tea party with me?"

"Not right now, Shannon, I'll come down in a little bit, okay?"

"Are you doing big-girl stuff?" Shannon asks, clearly not wanting to break the contact.

Molly heaves herself off the bed and opens the door as I stuff my one-piece back into my bag. Molly bends down to talk to Shannon, while the little girl peers eagerly into the bedroom. "Shanny, I'll be down in a little bit, okay? Why don't you have tea with your teddy bear and maybe share some with Luke until I come down?"

That seems to work, or maybe it's that she sees we're not doing anything exciting. Either way, little Shannon skips happily back down the stairs.

"Wow," says Molly, closing the door firmly behind her and pointing to my flea-market find. "That does *not* look comfortable."

"It's not *supposed* to be comfortable," I say, pulling the teddy back out of my bag. I am thoroughly annoyed with her know-it-all attitude—not one of her best traits. "It's just for show."

"It looks too . . . I dunno," she says, eyeing it with one finger on her chin. "Western, cowgirl, yee-haw . . . or something."

"What's wrong with that?" I ask. "A lot of guys go for that."

"Mike's not a lot of guys. He goes for you, and that is just not you," she says with certainty.

I spread the teddy out on the bed. "Then what would be 'me,' oh Wise Underwear Guru? Please enlighten."

She stands with one hand on her hip, throwing her head back to study her ceiling fan. "You need something classy, yet sleazy. Sophisticated, yet raunchy . . . *That* thing," she says, pointing a long French-tipped finger, "is all raunch. Which has its purposes, but not for his birthday."

"Then *what*?" I say, exasperated. I have completely run out of ideas, and Molly is my only hope.

"Something exciting, something *different* . . . something uniquely Samar Ahluwahlia."

"Okay, when you come up with it, I'll be right here," I say, lying back on her bed.

She taps her lips with the tip of her finger. "We need something out of the ordinary . . . maybe with an Eastern flavor."

"Excuse me—'Eastern flavor'? Like Cape Cod or Nantucket?"

"Hardy-har . . . no, you know—*Kama Sutra*, mantras, exotica . . . I bet that would be a huge hit with Mike." Molly's way more into my "Eastern" heritage than I am. It's not as if I'm *not* into it . . . it's just that it was never really into *me*.

My mom spent a whole lot of time, when I was growing up, smudging the hard lines that made us different from everyone around us. She dressed me like everyone else, packed my lunch with all the same snacks as the other kids, and stressed the fact that we're all more the same than different. "You're *American*," she'd say, "and that's all that matters. Don't let anyone tell you otherwise."

Molly digs through her closet and throws what looks like a bunch of lacy, silky rags on her bed. "Now that your uncle's coming around, you should mine that connection for nuggets we can use."

I groan. "First of all, Mike would rather I wear nothing. The frilly stuff is just a perk, as far as he's concerned. So, Western cowgirl, or 'Eastern flavor' is irrelevant. Secondly—yeah, I'll ask my *uncle* what I could use to turn my boyfriend on. Ew! You have a sick mind, Moll. Not to mention, my uncle blushes like a freakin' tomato when a Wonderbra commercial comes on."

She laughs. "Well, then, ask your mom," she says offhandedly. "If I had a hookup like that, I'd work it for all it's worth. Your culture gave you belly dancing, henna, body jewelry, and an entire *bible* of sexual positions, for Chrissake! What do I get? Four-leaf clovers and leprechauns."

"Even if my mom knew anything about any of that stuff, she would sure as hell not share it with me—not that I would want her to. She talks to me about sex, but sex in general . . . as in 'do whatever, but be safe.'"

Molly absently fingers the lace on a red bra. "That sucks," she says, flopping down next to me.

"Oh!" She jumps up and runs to her closet. She reaches into her secret compartment. "I almost forgot! The new Victoria's Secret catalogue came in the mail." She waves it in the air. "Ta-da! They're giving away a free tote bag when you buy a Body by Victoria bra—we *have* to go next Saturday!" She flips through the pages as we huddle together on her bed to pore over the catalogue.

"If I could have a body like Gisele, I'd never wear underwear," she says. "I'd just parade around town buck nekkit."

"You *do* have a body like Gisele's," I say, flipping the page. Molly's not as tall as Giselle, maybe, but she's fat in all the right places, and skinny in all the other right places. She's the very definition of cute, with freckles like raindrops across her cheekbones, and tight, apricot-colored corkscrew curls that spring up and down whenever she moves or shakes her head—which is a lot of the time. She does her own fashion thing, and most of her clothes are from thrift shops, or boutiques in New York City. The only thing she doesn't skimp on is sexy underwear.

"It's me who could use some of what she's got," I say.

"What are you talking about?" she says, looking me over and rolling her eyes in sheer disgust.

Even though we'd both love to be six-foot-tall Tyra- or Gisele-type runway material, we do okay. I'm five foot four, petite, with waist-length, loose curls that go ballistic when it's raining or humid out. I've had hairstyles that Buddhists could point to and say, "See? *That's* why we shave our heads."

"Oooooh, this is nice," Molly says, pointing to a picture of lace garters and thigh-high nylons. "I have something like this if you want to borrow it!" She rummages through her secret compartment—which is really a decorated shoe box from a second-grade school project—and comes back out with a similar outfit.

"I am not wearing that," I say, pointing to the garter belt, "but I will take the seam-up-the-back thigh-highs, thank you very much."

She hands them graciously to me. "Wear them *out*. And I expect a full and complete report, especially if my nylons have anything to do with you and Mike doing the Real Deal," she says, grinning.

"Mo-lly!" Her mom's voice coming up the stairs sends us scrambling for the lingerie pieces we've displayed all over the bed.

"Oh, crap," Molly mutters under her breath, shoving all the lace and satin back into its hiding spot. I yank out one of her textbooks. By the time Mrs. Mac knocks on the door, gone are Gisele and Tyra, and we're poring over one of Molly's three-inch-thick design books.

"Come in!" says Molly, in her sweetest singsong voice. Mrs. Mac opens the door and looks around the room.

She looks at the book in our hands and gives us a penetrating stare. "What are you girls doing?" she asks suspiciously. "There's a whole party going on downstairs. . . . Why are you two holed up in here?"

"Just needed a breather, Mom," Molly says innocently.

Her mother lingers in the doorway, looking around like some evidence of what we were *really* up to will make itself known. "Well, hurry up, then," she says finally. "We're about to cut the cake. You won't want to miss that!"

"We'll be right down, Mom!" Molly says as Mrs. Mac turns to go back down the stairs.

"Come on, Moll, let's go before she decides to come back."

She downs the rest of her drink. "Fine, but you have to fill me in on every single detail of birthday night."

"Deal," I say, draping an arm around her shoulders.

Mrs. Mac greets us with a wide smile as we reach the bottom of the stairs. "Sammy, will you be joining us for church next Sunday?"

Molly lets out an exasperated sigh as I fidget with the strap of my bag. "Um . . . uh . . ." Normally I make something up—I have a paper to write, or somewhere to go with my mom. But today I try a different tactic, one I never would have thought to use before.

"Thanks, Mrs. Mac, but I've decided to learn more about what it means to be Sikh." Molly raises her eyebrows and opens her mouth as if to speak, but closes it again without saying anything.

"Oh!" Mrs. Mac says in surprise. "Yes, well . . . the church is open to all. . . ."

"Thank you," I say, smiling brightly. I went to church once with Molly and her family, and Mom had a serious hissy fit.

If I'd gotten my nipple pierced like Andrea Bernstein's older sister did, Mom would have told me about hygienic needles and not dulling the sensitivity of the breasts—which is the talk I got anyway when I told her about Andrea's sister's nipple. If I'd gone to a bar and got trashed, she would have sat down to have a serious chat with me about responsible drinking and not walking home alone. But church? That's a whole different story. Mom's face flushed deep purple as she said, "Religion is for the mindless and ignorant. It's the opiate of the masses!"

Whatever. Either way, I wasn't crazy about sitting on a hard bench for what seemed like ages, and listening to a sermon on the sanctity of marriage. I kept thinking of all the things I would rather have been doing, like watching Mike do chin-ups in his boxers, or going shopping with Molly.

Molly giggles next to me and leans into my ear. "So, you've decided to 'learn more about being Sikh'?"

"Yeah," I say, a little more forcefully than intended. I bring my voice down a notch. "What's wrong with that?"

"Excuse me," Molly says, holding up her hands, "it's just that this is the first I've heard about it."

"So? Do you have to know every single thought that pops into my head?" I have no idea why I'm snapping at her, but I can't stop myself. Her know-it-all-ness is getting to me.

She looks hurt and I immediately want to apologize, but before I can say anything, Molly's aunt Aileen comes out of the kitchen carrying an enormous cake lit up like a July Fourth celebration. Everyone begins to sing "Happy Birthday" to Great-Aunt Maggie.

I mouth *sorry* to Molly.

She keeps singing, but gives me a "what's going on?" look.

I shake my head and stare at the candles on Great-Aunt

Maggie's froofy yellow cake. I don't know what to tell Molly, because I don't even know myself. But something about being in a room with so many people, so many *generations* that you belong to and who accept you without question as one of theirs, leaves me feeling like a hand is squeezing my heart, making it just a littler harder to breathe.

Chapter 3

The doorbell rings as Aunt Maggie's celebration is winding down. Uncle Sandeep is picking me and Molly up to take us back to my place to study for our Intro to Calculus quiz tomorrow. Since Molly's extended family has taken over her place, my house is ideal. Quiet, with no one there but Mom—and tonight, Uncle Sandeep.

He and Mom have been doing dinner once a week. It's the one night I look forward to having dinner at home. Otherwise, I make plans to be out, either at Molly's or at Mike's. But there's something about seeing the table set for three that makes dinner feel like an occasion at our house.

"Yes?" Molly's dad asks, opening the door. I hear a muffled voice outside asking for me. Mr. Mac turns to me in surprise. He points out the door with his thumb. "Know this guy, Sam?"

I forgot that this is the first time the MacFaddens, with the exception of Molly, are meeting Uncle Sandeep. I can't help the grin that spreads on my face. "That's my uncle," I say, getting up from my sunken spot on the sofa.

Mr. Mac steps aside to let Uncle Sandeep in. "Come on in," he says with an uncertain smile.

As I walk to the door, I notice a couple of people shooting glances at one another. "Uncle Sandeep," I say, all of a sudden feeling very uncomfortable, "this is Mr. MacFadden, Molly's dad. Mr. Mac, this is my Uncle Sandeep."

Before Mr. Mac has a chance to say anything, Molly's mom comes swooshing out of nowhere. "Well, don't just stand there, Sandy, come on in! There's plenty to drink and eat. What can I get you—beer, wine, a mixed drink?"

"No thank you, Mrs. MacFadden, I don't drink," Uncle Sandeep says, nodding his head.

"Well, how about juice, then?" Mrs. Mac says, steering Uncle Sandeep through the living room toward the kitchen.

I turn to follow them and notice Mr. Mac still watching Uncle Sandeep. As I walk through the living room amidst the laughter and conversation, I realize that several other pairs of eyes are trained on my uncle as well. Although most of the people in the room are still enjoying themselves, a few faces have become visibly taut.

For the first time in all the years I've known them, I feel self-conscious in the MacFaddens' home. Even though I've met almost everyone here at least once and I've always been treated like a member of the family, I feel like I'm being re-evaluated based on the latest evidence.

Part of me wants to say, "Um, I just met him . . . I don't really know him that well." And the other part wants to scream, "He's not a terrorist, okay?" Instead I clamp my jaw tight and walk stiffly into the kitchen. This feeling of being—and a jolt ricochets through my body as I think this—*unwelcome*, is like an echo, but as I try to zero in on it, it slips away.

Mrs. Mac chatters nonstop as she hands Uncle Sandeep a plastic cup with the same bubble-gum-flavored water she had handed me earlier.

He grimaces as he takes a sip. "I don't mean to intrude on your family celebration," he says, putting the cup down on the countertop. He turns to me meaningfully. "Samar, if you and Molly are ready to go now . . ."

As if on cue, Molly bounces in. "Uncle Sandeep, you're here!" She rushes him and throws her arms around his shoulders.

Uncle Sandeep smiles awkwardly, steps back, and untangles himself. "Hello, Molly. Are you two ready to go?"

Molly groans. "Ugh, calculus quiz first thing tomorrow morning!"

Mrs. Mac claps her hands. "Well, run along then, girls. Study, study, study!"

Molly and I grab our bags. But to my utter disbelief, Uncle Sandeep walks over to Great-Aunt Maggie to wish her a happy birthday. *What is he thinking?*

As soon as we get into his car, a sea-green Buick Regal, I click my seat belt in place and turn to Uncle Sandeep. "I thought you'd want to get out of there as soon as possible. I mean, was it me, or was there a . . . weird vibe going on as soon as you walked in?"

He sighs. "I'm used to it, Samar."

"What're you talking about?" Molly asks.

I turn around. "You didn't notice that several people in there were staring at Uncle Sandeep as soon as he set foot in the house?"

She frowns. "Well, they don't know him."

"None of them knew *me* the first time I met them, but they didn't shoot nervous glances at one another when I walked into the room."

Molly looks astonished. "You're a girl, he's a guy. It's different."

"You think that's what it was?"

The muscle at her jaw jumps. "What else?"

I look at Uncle Sandeep, who's staring out at the road. I turn back in my seat and say nothing.

After several moments of driving in silence, Uncle Sandeep clears his throat. "Seems as if your celebration was a big success, Molly."

Despite the frown, her face lights up. "Can you believe Great-Aunt Maggie is *ninety-two*?"

He shakes his head. "What's her secret?"

"She says to laugh every day and drink stout every night," Molly says with a smile.

Uncle Sandeep laughs. "Sounds like a fun lady."

Molly leans forward. "Thanks, Uncle Sandeep, she really is." I want to tell her that he is not her uncle, but I pull the words back. I've already had to apologize once this afternoon; I'm not doing it again.

"Everyone seems to have been having a good time," Uncle Sandeep says, smiling warmly at Molly in the rearview mirror.

"They always do," I say. "The MacFaddens always have a blast."

I didn't mean it as a compliment, but Molly reaches forward to tousle my hair. "Thanks, Sam," she says. "It's never as much fun when you're not around, though. You're part of our crew too, y'know."

I recall the numbing feeling that shot through my body at Molly's house. "It would be nice to have my own crew," I say, looking out the window.

"Hey," Uncle Sandeep says, "what am I—cherry pits?"

"It's chopped liver," says Molly, grinning. "And it's true, Sam. You do have your own crew."

I roll my eyes. "No offense, Uncle Sandeep, but one person, besides my mother, does not translate into a crew."

"It's a start," he says, looking hurt.

"I know, but . . ." I look out of the corner of my eye at Molly in the side mirror. "Look at the difference between the masses at Molly's and, and . . . *us.*"

Uncle Sandeep drives silently for a moment. When he comes to a stop at a red light, he turns to me. "I meant it's only a beginning, Sam. You do have a crew; a whole family— grandparents, cousins . . . your very own masses."

"Yes, but they're *crazy.* Mom says they're fanatics who don't want girls to cut their hair or shave their legs."

Uncle Sandeep raises his eyebrows. "She said *that*?"

I shrug. "Basically. Not in those words, maybe, but that's the gist."

He shakes his head, amazed. "God, she makes us sound like the Taliban."

"That's what I always pictured," I say, looking closer at his face. He shakes his head again.

He slows down at a stop sign and looks at me. "Do *I* fit that description?"

"You sure don't," Molly answers from the back. "From Sammy's descriptions all these years, I thought I'd be meeting Abdullah with his nine wives."

He smirks. "Wrong religion. Sikhs are not allowed more than one wife."

As we pull into our driveway, I can't get Uncle Sandeep's question out of my mind: *Do I fit that description?* No, he definitely does not fit the description that Mom always gave of her family. Not in the least. So what does that mean about the rest of Mom's family? The rest of *my* family? What are the Ahluwahlias like, if not miserable, critical, and controlling?

When we walk into the house, the smells of Mom's cooking hug us and fold us in. "Shoes off, everyone!" she says, waving a wooden spoon. Molly goes scurrying back to take off her boots. Although she's a regular visitor to the Ahluwahlia house, she forgets this rule every time.

"Coconut shrimp and green beans amandine," Mom announces.

"Can't wait to dig in," says Uncle Sandeep, washing his hands in the sink. "Will you girls be joining us?"

"Not me," Molly says. "I'm stuffed."

"Me either. Studying on the agenda," I say, heading up the stairs.

Molly follows me into my room and flops onto my bed. "I'm

tired," she complains. "I don't know how I'm going to focus on calculus!"

"No one told you to drink so much."

"I didn't drink 'so' much. I had a couple of social drinks at a birthday party." She rests her chin on one hand. "What's up with you, Wally? It's not like *you're* an angel."

Wally is the nickname Molly gave me when we were in second grade. We had just met and the other kids were taunting me, calling me Ahluwahli-ali-alia, or All-you-wallies. Mom and I had just moved into the neighborhood, and Molly and her family knew just about everyone. Molly started to affectionately call me Wally, and the teasing slowly fell off. I stuck to her like glue after that.

I stop leafing through my calc book. "Moll, are you honestly going to tell me you think those people were staring at Uncle Sandeep because he's a *guy*?"

She sits up, her mouth thinning into a straight line. "Sammy, if you're trying to say something, just say it."

I close my textbook. "You don't think the huge red turban on his head had anything to do with it?"

She throws her arms up. "It's because they don't know him, Sammy—he could've been wearing a potato sack! If some strange man walked into your house, wouldn't you stare?"

I shake my head as if to clear it. "Are you serious? I wouldn't stare if you told me he was your uncle!"

She climbs off the bed and stands in front of me with her arms crossed on her chest. "My family is *not* prejudiced."

I say nothing.

Color floods her face and her eyes glisten. "I can't believe you're saying this, Sammy—you've known us forever! When have we ever made you feel . . ." Her voice fades, and she stares at me for a moment. Then she snaps up her books and calmly marches out of my room. I make no move to stop her.

I hear her footsteps, followed by Mom's and Uncle Sandeep's surprised voices, then the front door slamming shut.

A few moments later, Mom's at my door. "Sammy, what happened?"

"Nothing."

She fixes me with a hard stare. "Samar, you two have had your spats in the past," she says, then points downstairs, "but Molly has never stormed out of here like that. Don't tell me it was nothing."

I open my textbook. "Mom, I don't want to talk about it, okay?"

She stands there without saying anything. "Fine," she says finally, turning around. "But good friends aren't easy to find, Sam. Keep that in mind."

Whatever. What would she know about friends and family? The only family she ever had she dumped, and maybe for no reason. She has no friends—just a few "gal pals" to go out with every now and then. And if Uncle Sandeep hadn't come back around, she never would have made the effort to contact *him*.

I hear the murmur of voices downstairs as the equations and numbers in my textbook merge and blur together. How could Molly not see it? If the people at her house this afternoon got to know Uncle Sandeep, they'd love him. But a lot of those faces looked like they had already made up their minds. Maybe the same way I'd made up my mind about Mom's family and about Uncle Sandeep, based on the few words she'd given me.

I hang my head. Why didn't I ever think to find out for myself? I snap my textbook shut. Some things are more important than calculus. Like figuring out how I'm going to meet the rest of my very own crew—beginning with Mom's parents.

When I get home from school on Monday, I ask Mom if I can hang out with Mike for a bit.

She gives me a look. "It's a weeknight, Sammy." Mom's fine with me dating, but she has never really been crazy about Mike. She hasn't come right out and admitted it, but it's pretty easy to tell when Mom doesn't like someone.

My voice heads into whine country. "I know, but I never get to see him anymore, and Molly's totally incommunicado."

"You two haven't worked that out yet?"

"Mom!"

She purses her lips. "What about your homework?"

"It's totally manageable." Not completely true, but close enough.

She sighs. "I suppose, but be back by dinner."

I race upstairs to call Mike.

About half an hour later I hear the doorbell. When I come down the stairs, Mom and Mike are exchanging awkward small talk just inside the doorway. Mike, at six foot three, towers over Mom's five foot one.

"Hey," I say, a little breathless. I stand on my tiptoes and kiss his cheek. No mouth kisses in front of Mom—she's cool about dating and all, but not *that* cool.

"Hey," he says. "Ready?"

"Ready. Bye, Mom," I toss over my shoulder.

"What's up?" Mike asks, once we've turned the corner.

"Mama drama," I say, flipping through his CDs.

He reaches for my hand.

"She's so nosy! Molly and I had a fight yesterday, and Mom's all over me about it."

"What did you fight about?"

I find a Joss Stone CD and pop it in the player. "Uncle Sandeep picked me up at her place and there was this weird vibe, and she just wouldn't admit it!"

"A weird vibe?"

"I don't know . . . it was just this weird feeling. . . ."

He nods but doesn't say anything.

"Plus, he and Mom have been talking about a lot of family stuff since he came around."

"Hmm," he says. "Probably some serious stuff."

"That's it, exactly," I say, a bit too forcefully. "I think I do need to find out more about my family—my history."

"Why?"

I exhale in exasperation. "What do you mean, *why*? Because I don't know anything about them!"

"Take it easy, babe." He reaches across the seat to take my hand. "I'm only asking because you've always seemed fine with it being just you and your mom."

I lean back against the seat for a moment. "I'm sorry. I didn't mean to snap. It's just that . . . I don't know. Something about Uncle Sandeep coming back makes me want to know more, you know? Maybe I could be part of something bigger—a family, community . . . *something*. Does that make sense?"

He looks thoughtful as he stares out at the road ahead. "I guess," he says.

"Whenever I'm at Molly's with her big family gatherings, I feel like it's a club, or a secret society that has its own words and meanings, and I never quite fit in . . . totally. And I felt it so much more yesterday when Uncle Sandeep came to get me." I glance over at him. "I'm sorry, I don't want to go on about my problems. I don't expect you to understand."

He cocks his head to one side. "Maybe I do. Give me a chance. Is it like walking into a loving family and thinking only of your own family's brokenness? Or like going to a restaurant with your college friends and not being able to order anything from the menu because you're paying off your mom's credit cards?"

I wince. I've been so absorbed in my own problems that I completely forgot what Mike has to deal with every day. Suddenly I feel like a selfish kid. "Kinda," I say softly, looking at his profile. "I don't mean to go on about all my crap."

He gives my hand a squeeze.

"I don't really get the restaurant comparison, though."

He smiles. "You walk in thinking you're the same as everyone else, only to realize you're *not*. Nobody understands what you gotta deal with. They're in their cushy worlds and you're the kid outside the window."

"Wow. That's *exactly* what I mean."

He winks and kisses the inside of my wrist as we pull into his driveway.

The part of town where Mike lives has more apartment buildings and townhouses than where I live. In my neck of the woods, all the houses have lawns and backyards. Streets end in "Crescent" or "Circle" or "Lane." I live on Riverview Lane, and Molly lives a few streets down on Walnut Crescent.

From the outside of Mike's home, you'd never think the inside looks the way it does. His mom likes the finer things in life and has gone into debt to get them. She's almost never home, so most of the time we have the place to ourselves, which is really convenient for make-out sessions. It's always too warm at his place, and Mike puts on one of his jazz or R & B CDs, and we cocoon ourselves away from parents and school, and now (for him) work.

We walk in and fling our jackets onto the dining room chairs, letting them stay wherever they land.

"Want something to drink?"

I nod, sinking into the cream-colored leather sofa.

"What's new at school?" he asks, coming back and setting a Coke in front of me.

I take a sip. "Lots of talk about September eleventh."

"Yeah. That's all anybody ever talks about at work, too. All day long."

"I have to do a paper for Lesiak on it, and we're talking about it in American history."

He guzzles half of his Coke. "Those bastards came out of their caves and ruined innocent lives for *nothing*."

I turn to stare at him, my stomach beginning to churn. "But, but . . . we don't really know what happened, Mike. . . ."

He jerks his head around to look at me, eyes wide, incredulous. "What do you mean, *we don't know what happened*? You saw it all on TV, didn't you? Everyone in the whole goddamn world saw it! Thousands of people died for no friggin' reason, Sam."

I bury my face into my hands. "I saw it," I mumble.

I feel him move onto the floor in front of me and wedge himself between my knees. He runs his fingers through my hair. "Sorry, babe."

When I look up, he's facing me with his elbows on my thighs. I stare into his eyes—green with gold and black specks, like a kiwi cut across the equator.

"Had a crappy day at work today. My deadbeat dad called my mom, and off she ran to meet him again. Always amazes me how she can forget the twenty thousand dollars of credit card debt *I'm* helping her climb out of while he sits in bars every night."

I caress his shoulders. He looks so tired. Ever since he got promoted to manager at Tools 'N' Tires, a retail chain hardware store, he looks less and less like the Mike he was last year when we were in school together. Over the summer he started to walk around like all the things his mom bought on credit were piled up on his shoulders.

"Come on," he says, getting up. "Let's pop in a DVD. What do you want to watch?"

"I have to be home for dinner," I remind him.

"We'll make it."

We watch an Adam Sandler movie and cuddle on the couch the rest of the afternoon.

Chapter 4

By Thursday I have two plans. Two promising plans.

Plan A is simple: Persuade Mom to reconnect with her family. Uncle Sandeep is key in this plan. If it doesn't work, I move to Plan B: Tell Mom nothing and convince Uncle Sandeep to take me to meet my grandparents. For both of the aforementioned plans to move forward smoothly, I need to do a bit of gardening. I need to dig deep to uncover some roots—*my* roots. And then there's Plan C: If neither of these plans works, come up with a Plan C.

I rush around getting ready for school and go over ways to approach Mom—and the possible outcomes. None of them are good. Especially since I caught a piece of Mom and Uncle Sandeep's conversation last night:

"Sharan, just think about it. You haven't seen Ma and Papa in years! They've grown since then."

"Ha! They wouldn't know the meaning of the word! Forget it, Sandeep, they're *toxic*."

Okay, so I've got my work cut out for me. But I've got Uncle Sandeep on my side, and Mom might surprise us both. Right?

Sure. Still, I've got to try. If I really give it a good shot, I could have my *own* huge family celebration by the holidays. No more squidging myself into Molly's family celebrations.

I hear a car horn and quickly coat mascara on my lashes. "Sammy! Mike's outside!" Mom calls from the bottom of the stairs.

"Coming!" I fumble through my makeup case for the Brandywine lipliner and Island Sunset lipstick. Another, longer honk.

"Saaaammy!"

"I'm coming, I'm *coming*," I grumble, and race down the stairs.

I give Mom a quick air kiss. "Remember, I'm hanging out with Mike later tonight!"

"What? Did we discuss this?" she says, looking up from her morning schedule.

I sit on a chair to pull on my boots. "Mom—it's Mike's birthday!"

"Is that today? Didn't you already see him this week? What are you two doing?"

I huff and heave myself up to pull the door open. I know Mike's probably having a cow by now. "We're just staying in and probably watching a movie or something."

"What did you get him?"

"Mom, I have to go!" I wave without looking back and run out the door.

I climb into his baby—his Honda Civic, and he gives me his "what the hell?" look.

"Sorry." I lean in for a kiss.

He gives me a quick peck on the corner of my mouth and roars into reverse, peeling out of the driveway.

"Jeez! Take it easy," I say, fumbling with my seat belt.

"Sammy, you can't be late *every* time I pick you up for school!" he says, driving with one hand on the wheel, the other adjusting the heat level. "I have to be at work, I can't fart around anymore."

"No one says you have to pick me up." I pull down the sun visor to put my lipstick on. "I'm gonna be at school an hour early. I could very easily take the bus with Molly, y'know." I haven't told him about the Molly situation yet.

"Yeah, yeah," he grumbles. "It's not bad enough that I don't get to see you all day anymore. Now I have to compete with Molly and Uncle."

I finish lining my lips, mostly to chill out before I say anything. "He has a name."

"Oh, sorry. What is it? Uncle So-deep? Or is it Some-deep?" He snickers.

"It's Uncle *Sandeep*. Cut it out, Mike. What's wrong with you?" I hate it when he gets like this. It has been happening more and more lately. He gets mean and cold and bitter without warning, like something just sets him off.

He shakes his head. "I just think it's weird that you meet the guy less than two months ago, and now you're real tight. Where's he been all this time?"

"It's not his fault. My mom didn't want to see him. Look, whatever—just call him by his name, okay?"

"Yeah, yeah," he says, turning down the street to Melville High.

My neck is tight, but I drop it. I keep hoping the real Mike, the one I met and used to have fun with, the cute, popular, jokester Mike, will come back full-time; that maybe being with me and remembering what things were like before will make him click back somehow.

I take a deep, controlled breath in and let it out slowly. I don't want to fight with Mike on his birthday.

"Besides," I say, turning to him with a truce-smile, "you'd be in college if you weren't working, and we still wouldn't see each other."

"I wouldn't be in college because I wouldn't have the money to be in college."

Last year when we discussed which of the local colleges we would all apply to, Mike told me and Molly he was postponing college altogether. He said it would only be for a year or so, to help his mom out with the bills. Molly and I made him swear that it would be temporary. But it doesn't seem to be on the horizon at all anymore.

He shrugs and fiddles with the CD player. The voice of Ludacris explodes a minute later. I reach over to turn it down.

He reaches to turn it back up, but not to the level it was before.

I lean back in my seat and stare at the roof of the car. "Happy birthday," I say softly.

He relaxes his shoulders for a second and reaches across to grab my hand. I see a flash of soft Mike, the all-alone Mike with the baby seal eyes. He brings my knuckles to his lips.

I smile, pointing to the CD player. "You heard me over all that?"

He winks. "Loud and clear, babe."

"So, what do you want to do tonight?"

He doesn't let go of my hand. "I dunno . . . surprise me."

He pulls into the parking lot of the school, and I unbuckle my seatbelt. "You got it, see you tonight."

He leans in for a kiss. "I'll swing by after work."

I give him a quick peck, wave, and slam the door. Then I walk toward the white, blocky building that is Melville High. I open the double doors and get blasted with a wall of heat. I go to my locker to drop off my books and backpack, then grab a pack of gum and walk to the unofficial smoking section in the back of the school.

Even though neither of us smokes, the smoking section is where Molly and I sometimes hang out. It's a forgotten corner of the school that rarely gets patrolled, and students loiter freely, any time of day—even when they should be in class.

It's seven o'clock in the morning, and daylight is anything but broad in the remote back corner. In this town in late October, the trees are already gray, poking into a dreary, slate gray sky. I huddle against the wall on a cement block that a couple of stoners propped up in place of a bench. I pop a stick of gum into my mouth and open my calculus text. But the only thing I can think of is arguments to use on Mom for reconnecting with her parents.

This plan isn't something I'd share with Mike—he wouldn't understand. His whole family is here, but he doesn't care if he ever sees them. I sigh and shut my textbook again. Another quiz I'm not studying for. Mom says I'm too smart for my own good, and it's making me lazy. It's true that I almost never study for tests, but somehow, miraculously, the answers come to me when the test is in front of me. Good thing, too, because Lim is one of those teachers who likes to pop quizzes on students at least three times a week. I sit like that for close to an hour—not studying calculus and instead, searching for ways to fine-tune my plan.

The double doors open. Balvir Virk, who took Latin with me and Molly last year, comes out. She's wearing a skintight, blazing-red leather skirt with matching lipstick. Her hair is blown out and her eyes are lined in retro eighties style, like comets with tails going almost up into her temples.

"Hey," she says.

"Hey."

"Can I bum some gum?" she asks hesitantly.

"Sure." I extend the open pack. "What're you doing here so early?"

She pops the gum into her mouth, then lights a cigarette. She takes a long, deep drag. She smirks. "You think I leave the house looking like this?"

I give her a blank stare.

She laughs. "I leave the house looking like an Indian-American nun. Only to emerge—voilà!—into the smokers' corner looking like this." She twirls around.

"You do all that here?" I say, pointing to the school building.

She nods. "I'm fast. Me and a few other girls get here around a quarter of eight. Do you know Priya?" I shake my head. "Manavi?" Again I shake my head. "Belinder?"

"Nope."

She half shrugs and takes another drag.

I'm intrigued. I had always glanced over her in Latin class. Who knew she had all this going on? A couple of times I had heard Bobbi Lewis whisper behind her hand that Balvir looked like a cross between a clown and a hooker.

Molly and I are well liked, but Bobbi Lewis is in a whole other stratosphere. She drives to school in her own pink Lexus. I never said anything to Bobbi and instinctively veered away from Balvir. It's social suicide to be friends with anyone that Bobbi Lewis has dissed. I swallow the sudden lump of shame in my throat.

"It sucks that you have to bring a change of clothes to school every day," I say, and notice her wince slightly.

She looks off into the field. "Yeah, you're really lucky you don't have to." Then she turns to me. "Are you from Trinidad or Guyana . . . ?"

Despite my very Indian name, most of the Indian kids at school assume I'm not Indian because . . . well, I don't really know *exactly* why. Maybe it's because I don't hang out with them, or other Indian kids, anywhere—maybe that comes out of my pores, like a smell. And because I don't hang out with the West Indian kids either, I kind of get lumped into this weird place where I don't really fit anywhere.

"My mom was born in India."

She raises her eyebrows, exhaling a stream of smoke. "No shit," she says. "Your dad, too?"

I nod.

She flicks her cigarette and shakes her head. "I never would've guessed."

At one time a comment like that might've made me proud. But for some reason, now I bristle. "What do you mean?"

"I'm sorry, I didn't mean that to sound . . ." She drops her cigarette butt on the ground and stubs it out with her spike-heeled boot. "I mean, I knew you had some Indian in you *somewhere*, but I figured you were something else—Indo-Caribbean, Dominican, Puerto Rican, mixed. . . ." She peers at me from underneath hooded eyes and shrugs. "Or else you were a coconut."

"A coconut?" I've been mistaken for Dominican and everything else she listed, but a coconut?

"Yeah, you know . . . brown on the outside, white on the inside."

That catches me off guard. In grade school I was called plenty of names—*paki, doo-doo skin* . . . all kinds of things to let me know my brown skin was not coveted. This is the first time someone's telling me I'm not brown *enough*. It's true I've always been like the center of a daisy, if daisies had dark centers. Surrounded by all these white petals: Molly, my best friend, and her family; Mike, my boyfriend, and his buddies; and just about everyone else except Mom.

But that's because whenever I tried to hang out with the Indian kids at school, they talked about things I knew nothing about, sometimes using words in languages other than English—which is the only language I'm fluent in. Things always got real awkward real fast when we realized we had nothing much to talk about other than school. In some ways, that was even harder than the obvious differences between me and the white folks I surrounded myself with.

I'm still reeling when she opens the door. "Thanks for the gum," she says. "See ya!"

My brain is vibrating as I walk to calculus, and math is nowhere in the mix. I take my usual seat by the window and stare at my closed textbook. By now I know there's no use even trying to concentrate.

Molly walks in, smiling. Even though we left on bad terms on Sunday, and she has spent a lot of energy the past few days ignoring me to death, I could really use my best friend right now. I'm about to smile and wave, when I realize she's not smiling at me. On her heels is Bobbi Lewis—the same Bobbi Lewis that we've hated since third grade. They find seats on the other side of the room. Together.

My world is crumbling. I can feel the tremor like an actual earthquake.

The bell rings and Mr. Lim rushes in. Immediately, he starts distributing the quiz. He places it facedown on everyone's desk.

"Please don't turn your paper over until I give the okay," he says, looking at the clock. "You have exactly fifteen minutes to complete this quiz. When you are finished, turn your paper over on your desk and I will collect it. Please remember all quizzes count toward twenty-five percent of your final grade." He looks at the class. "Any questions?" He gives the room a quick, sweeping glance, then nods. "Good. Begin."

There is a brief rustling of papers. I turn mine over and all the questions come into sharp focus. For fifteen minutes, I think of nothing but integrals, derivatives, functions, and tangents.

I finish just as Lim announces time's up. I look over at Molly. Her test is still faceup on her desk, and she's busy counting something out on her fingers. In front of her, Bobbi leans back in her seat and messes with one of her French-tipped fingernails.

Once all the tests are collected, Lim introduces a new lesson for the rest of the period, while I try to keep my head from swiveling back in Molly's direction. She, on the other hand, acts like I've fallen off the planet.

The teacher finally writes that night's homework on the board and I quickly jot it down in my notebook. When I look up, I see that most of the class has gone, including Molly and Bobbi. I feel as if I'm hurtling back in time to second grade, when I stood alone in the schoolyard. A time when *paki* and *doo-doo skin*, *Ahlu-wahli-ali-alia* and *all-you-wallies* rang clear and sharp, slicing through me to a deep, soft center.

I walk slowly to my next class, AP English. I'm in no hurry to get there because Balvir is in that class with me. Her coconut remark still stings.

Am I? Could I really be what she said? A *coconut*. Spat out the same way as *doo-doo skin*.

I walk into Ms. Lesiak's English class, taking a seat as far away from Balvir as possible.

Since September eleventh was a week after school started,

Ms. Lesiak and many other teachers have themed assignments around "recovering" and "moving forward." Ms. Lesiak is big on generating Healthy Discussion and Debate. For her class, the assignment is to write about the impact of the World Trade Center attacks on our lives.

I get a huge clenching in my belly every time the topic is brought up. Snapshots of the smoking towers flash through my head along with all the other images from that day. I take a few deep breaths and focus, instead, on going over things I need to learn and find out—if my plan is to go smoothly. (1) I need to learn more about Sikhism. (2) I need to learn more about Indian-ness, specifically Punjabi-ness, and maybe Uncle Sandeep could even teach me a few words in Punjabi.

I start scribbling notes about where I might get some of my information. I remember to look up every now and then to nod seriously, like I'm in deep contemplation about the occasional nuggets of wisdom that drop from Lesiak's mouth.

I tune back in for a moment when Balvir reads one of her poems aloud:

". . . fear, anger, rage/dripping like acid from an IV. Sound bites and video clips/television screens showing pieces of people/living in a censored/sensory world/elaborate tales spun into explanations."

After she sits down, the only sound is the *chunk-chunk* of the enormous wall clock.

Then Shazia Azem, who rarely says anything in any of the classes I have with her, now speaks up in a surprisingly strong and deep voice. "But why? Why would anyone do that?

This is not the work of a deranged crazy person. These were well-educated, intelligent men who were deeply dedicated to a cause. In their countries, they might be considered freedom fighters. . . ."

"They're religious fanatics," says David Eng. "There's tons of those in the world. And some of the most brutal serial killers were educated, smooth-talking dudes."

Melanie Castell speaks from the back of the class. "I hope we lock them all up and throw away the key."

"But who's 'them'?" Adam Dodic asks without raising his hand. "I mean, is 'them' Al-Qaeda? People from Afghanistan? Iraq? The whole Middle East?"

"All Muslims?" Shazia adds.

David Eng nods his head. "And there's been terrorism in Ireland, Oklahoma, Bosnia . . ."

Ken Ruiz, who has been jiggling his leg the whole time in the seat next to me, says, "I think it's horrible, our policies in the Middle East—don't get me wrong, I love Jesus and everything. And what those people did on September eleventh was horrible, but we still have to stop fighting and killing each other over oil over there."

Balvir turns to look at the rest of the class and ends up looking directly at me, her face hopeful, as if I might be an ally. "But still . . . there has to be more to the story than what we're getting on the news, don't you think?"

I wish I could answer, but I don't know what to think. I swallow hard and look down at my list of "Things to Learn about My Culture." Then I look at my "List of Resources" next to it: *Internet, library, Uncle Sandeep.* And the last line I jotted down: *Where to start?!?*

For the first time ever in a classroom setting, I feel stupid. Like a mixture of doo-doo skin, coconut, and bonehead, all rolled up into a lump.

Chapter 5

Molly spends all day pointedly ignoring me, while being hermetically sealed to Bobbi Lewis's armpit. By the end of the day, I can't take it anymore. I grab my books from my locker and sprint to hers before she has a chance to duck out.

When I round the corner, she's slamming her locker shut and searching the halls. I almost run her over in my hurry.

"Hey," I say, breathless. She gives me a look that could refreeze melting polar ice caps, and continues searching the halls.

"Moll—come on, we're best friends."

"We *were* best friends," she says, icing me with her eyes.

"We still are, Moll." I'm almost pleading. I lower my voice. "You've got to be sick of Bobbi by now."

She juts her chin out. "Bobbi happens to be a great friend."

My jaw unhinges. "Since when?"

"And she's not a reverse racist, like you."

"A *what*?"

Just then Molly stands on her tiptoes, waving madly. I turn

to look over my shoulder, and Bobbi, looking like bronzed caramel with waist-length extensions, rounds the bend with a couple of her ladies-in-waiting. I feel the breeze as Molly rushes past me. I stand rooted to the spot, my mouth still open.

When I finally clear my head and look around, they're all out of sight. I walk slowly toward the exit. *A reverse racist?* She can't be serious! And Bobbi Lewis—a *great friend?* No way. Molly has either gone bonkers, or she's really trying to piss me off. And knowing her like I do, it has to be the latter.

When I come out into the sunlight, I pull my coat tighter around my neck. I notice that a few lone brown leaves still cling to swaying branches. I hook my thumbs through the straps of my backpack, then freeze.

At the bottom of the hill, Molly and Bobbi are giggling and in animated conversation with someone in a car. Someone in a sea-green Buick Regal, someone wearing a crimson turban.

My ears pound as I get closer. Molly morphs into the Ice Queen as soon as she sees me, and Bobbi inspects her manicure.

"Samar! I thought I would pick you up today, and look who I ran into—your friends Molly and Bobbi!"

I shove my hands into my pockets and say nothing. I know if I dare speak now, it'll only come out as incoherent sputtering. Uncle Sandeep looks at my face, then at the other girls, and scrunches up his eyebrows. He nods, as if he just solved an equation.

"Girls," he says to Molly and Bobbi, "can Samar and I give you a lift somewhere?"

"No, thanks," Bobbi says, tilting her head to one side and smiling a dimpled smile. "I have my car in the lot." She turns to Molly and gives her an air kiss on one cheek. "See you tomorrow, chica." She gives me a half nod and bounces away.

Molly looks only at Uncle Sandeep. "Thanks, but I'd rather walk, Uncle Sandeep."

Again I have the sudden urge to tell her he is *not* her uncle—she has a million of her own to choose from. But instead I walk around to the passenger side and get in. Thank God she didn't say yes.

"Oh, come on, Molly," Uncle Sandeep says. "You're on the way, and it's getting rather chilly now. It's only a few moments in the car—you'll be home before you know it."

Molly looks at me and purses her lips. She looks back at Uncle Sandeep and seems to consider the offer. I hold my breath. *Don't get in, don't get in, don't get in. . . .*

"You're right—it is a pretty quick ride . . ."

Don't get in, don't get in. . . .

"Okay, I'll get in." She climbs in, slams the door, and buckles her seat belt, while I grind my teeth.

Uncle Sandeep darts glances alternately at me and at Molly in the rearview mirror.

"How was school?" he asks, looking at neither of us in particular. I look in the side mirror on the passenger door and see Molly open her mouth to speak.

I blurt out, "Molly made a new friend."

She closes her mouth.

I can tell she's wishing she never got in. Good.

Uncle Sandeep raises his eyebrows and looks in the rearview mirror at Molly. "Is that so?"

"Bobbi is not a new friend," she says tersely. "Samar and I have known Bobbi almost as long as we've known each other. We just never bothered to get to know her better."

I shake my head and turn around. "Excuse me?"

Uncle Sandeep nods earnestly.

"Yes, it's very important to give people the benefit of the doubt," he says. "You never know how much you might have in common with another person unless you put your fears aside. Good for you, Molly."

Molly nods gravely. "Yeah, I'm glad I gave her a chance."

I'm floored. I want to bang some cymbals together and wake Molly up from her delusional fantasy. "*Fears?* 'Gave her a chance'? We weren't *afraid* of Bobbi Lewis—she's a stuck-up rich girl who thinks she's better than everyone else! At least that's what *Molly* said earlier this year."

"Maybe it's time to grow up," she shoots back. "Maybe some of us are ready to move on and up."

On and up?!?

Uncle Sandeep rounds a corner. I begin to fire a smart comment back when something loud thuds against Uncle Sandeep's door. He swerves into oncoming traffic and swerves quickly back into his own lane. Another couple of thuds, then a loud clanging sound as something hits the rear window.

"Duck down, girls!" Uncle Sandeep shouts.

"What the hell is that?" Molly yells from behind. I crane my neck to see what's happening. An earthquake? A tornado?

What I see is three guys standing on one side of the road, pelting debris at Uncle Sandeep's car. They hurl bags of garbage and soda cans from the curb.

Uncle Sandeep rolls down his window. "Stop—wait!" he yells.

"Go back home, Osama! No bombs on civilians here, asshole, this is America!"

I sit up, my body vibrating like a guitar string. I recognize those voices. They're Rick Taylor, Chuck Banfield, and Simon Monroe. Guys I've known since grade school, whose voices make me want to run. Rick Taylor and Chuck Banfield ambushed me regularly in second grade, before I started hanging out with the right people—namely Molly and her friend Anna, before Anna moved away to Hawaii.

Molly's eyes are wider than mine. "What the f—!" she breathes, then darts a look at Uncle Sandeep. "What the hell are those guys *thinking*?"

Uncle Sandeep shakes his head as he whizzes through traffic and speeds away. "Nothing new," he says, glancing back over his shoulder. "The last couple of months have been like this."

"Why would they do that? Why would they call you Osama? You're not anything like him . . . you didn't *do* anything!" Molly says in astonishment. I breathe deep. My nails are digging into the seat.

"Tell *them* that," Uncle Sandeep says, pointing his thumb behind us. "Sikhs, Muslims, Arabs, Indians—it's all the same to those guys." He takes a shaky breath. "I understand the fear and suspicion, but this"—he waves around the car—"this is unnecessary!"

I finally find my voice and screech, "Why did you open your window? You could've been hit in the head by a soda can, or . . . worse!"

"I had to say *something*, Samar. They're ignorant, those fellows." He flips on the windshield wipers to clear some of the dirt from the windshield. "The only antidote to ignorance is education."

I gawk at him. "So you wanted to give them a *lesson*? Do you think they care?"

"I have to do something. I can't simply sit here and be afraid; they would think they've won."

It suddenly strikes me as funny that Uncle Sandeep is talking about not being afraid and not letting "them" win. Exactly the same thing I've been hearing on the TV about the terrorists. If I wasn't so freaked out, I might laugh at the weirdness of it all.

"I'm with Sammy on this one," Molly says, looking shaken up. "I'd keep my windows up and drive real fast. They've never done anything to me, but I once saw those guys drive a nail through the shell of a live turtle just to see if they could."

Uncle Sandeep pulls into Molly's driveway and whips his head around to look at her. "You know them?" he asks, a note of dread in his voice.

Molly and I nod. "Since grade school," I say.

"You girls be careful," he says passionately. "They've seen you in this car with me." He gives me a desperate look. "Don't walk home alone, Samar. Always make sure you are not alone!"

"Don't worry, Uncle Sandeep," Molly says, leaning forward

and putting a hand on my shoulder. "Sammy won't be walking alone."

He gives her a wobbly smile. "Good," he says, "very good."

My eyes fill. I want to say something to Molly, but I know I'll unravel if I do. She gathers her bags. "See you tomorrow, Sam." I nod, blinking back my tears.

When we get home, Mom is already upstairs, finished with her clients for the day. One look at my face and she flies to my side. "What happened, Sandeep?" she says sharply.

"Take a look at the car," he says, shaking his head.

Mom walks over to the window.

"My God!" she breathes. "Were you in an accident?"

"It was no accident," I say, collapsing into a chair and unlacing my boots.

Mom's eyes harden as understanding seeps in. "We'll file a police report," she says firmly.

Uncle Sandeep walks to a seat and sinks into it. He puts his head in his hands. "Sharan, I've filed so many police reports . . . they must have a binder full by now."

Mom explodes. "There must be something we can do! At least on the grounds of property damage, if nothing else, no? We can't just let them get away with this!"

"Nothing was damaged, Sharan . . . just ended up with a dirty car." He looks up at her with a puzzled expression. "You act as if this is something new, as if we didn't grow up with it."

She wrings her hands. "The name-calling, bullying . . . the schoolyard fights, yes. But for me and Sammy it hasn't been the way it was when you and I were growing up; we've had far fewer incidents of this kind . . . at least until—"

"Until I came along," he says softly. "This is what you ran away from. And here I am, bringing it all back to your doorstep."

Mom doesn't meet his eyes. "Sandeep, we've spoken about this ad nauseum. I left because I couldn't breathe. I felt like hands were around my throat, day in and day out. I left because that"—she points out the window to Uncle Sandeep's car—"was going on at school, and at home I wasn't allowed to have a single free thought!"

"And all these years everything's been fine because you could pretend you don't belong to us." He stands up. "You could run away, fit in, and cloak your differences—become an upstanding assimilated American."

"Careful," Mom says, her voice deadly calm.

"No, Sharan, you've had your say about Ma and Papa and me." He walks to his coat and boots. "Why doesn't Samar speak a stitch of Punjabi? Why has she no clue about her family? What does she know about her history, the struggles of her people?"

Mom's hands clench at her sides. "I think you'd better leave now."

"Fine," he says, "but you need to hear it. Samar deserves better." He looks at me. His lashes are wet. "Bye, Samar. You have my cell number—call me if you need anything at all."

I nod, feeling like I'm being torn to shreds.

Mom bangs things around in the kitchen after Uncle

Sandeep leaves, then gives up. "Can you just fend for yourself tonight, Sam? I'm tired," she says with her back to me.

Fine by me. Sitting through dinner with her right now would be like Chinese water torture, slow and maddening.

I go upstairs and sit down at my desk. But my uncle's words play a game of tag through my brain: *This is what you ran away from. . . . You could pretend you don't belong to us.* I open a textbook to study, but the words jump in and out of my mind like puppies in a box. *Why doesn't Samar speak a stitch of Punjabi? Why has she no clue about her family?*

I close the textbook and log on to my computer. I go immediately to Google. I type in "Sikh history" and get 158,392 listings. I click on the first one: a site with a squiggly character in 3-D and the phrase "One Creator. Universal Equality." scrolling across the top. Two minutes into reading about the ten guru prophets, my computer shuts down. I growl, boot it back up, and go to a different site.

On *religioustolerance.org*, I find:

> *Sikhism was founded by Shri Guru Nanak Dev Ji (1469–1538). At Sultanpur, he received a vision to preach the way to enlightenment and God. He taught a strict monotheism, the brotherhood of humanity. He rejected idol worship, and the oppressive Hindu concept of caste.*

> *The name of the religion means "learner." It is often mispronounced "seek." It should be*

pronounced "se-ikh," with the final kh *sound like the* kh *in Mikhail Gorbachev.*

Huh. Mom always pronounces it "seek," but Uncle Sandeep says it the way you'd say "sick," but with a harder *k* sound . . . I guess that's what they meant by the Mikhail Gorbachev thing. I go back to the Google listings and click on another site, allaboutsikhs.com.

Over twenty million Sikhs follow a revealed, distinct, and unique religion born five centuries ago in the Punjab region of northern India. Between 1469 and 1708, ten Gurus preached a simple message of truth, devotion to God, and universal equality. Often mistaken as a combination of Hinduism and Islam, the Sikh religion can be characterized as a completely independent faith. . . .

Sikhism . . . recognizes the equality between both genders and all religions. . . . Sikhs have their own holy scripture, Guru Granth Sahib. Written, composed, and compiled by the Sikh Gurus themselves, the Guru Granth Sahib serves as the ultimate source of spiritual guidance for Sikhs. . . .

I'm so absorbed in what I'm reading that when my cell phone buzzes next to me, I almost scream. I flip it open. Mike.

"Hey," I say, making my voice as normal as possible.

"I'm on my way," he says. I hesitate for a moment, not wanting to stop reading. Between everything that happened on the way home from school and the fight between Uncle Sandeep and Mom, the heat and excitement I felt about tonight has deflated quite a bit.

"Still there?"

I try to muster up some enthusiasm. "Mm-hmm, yeah, I'm still here. Okay, see you soon."

I hang up and look around in a daze. How do I go through an evening with Mike without telling him what's going on? I don't want to be a downer on his birthday, yet it's almost all I can think about right now. In my head, the words I've been reading on my computer screen compete for air time with Uncle Sandeep's words—*What does she know about her history?*

Okay, pull it together, Sammy.

I rifle through my closet. I'm no longer in the mood for Molly's thigh-highs. I pull on a short skirt, black nylons with a tiger at the ankles, and a tight black sweater. Mike's favorite outfit. The sweater is itchy as hell, but I'll deal with it for tonight. *You could cloak your differences . . . become an upstanding assimilated American.* I'm shivering, but I can't tell if it's from the cold or the nuclear blasts detonating in my brain. *It should be pronounced "se-ikh," with the final* kh *sound like the* kh *in Mikhail Gorbachev.*

Mike honks his horn outside. As I hurry down the stairs, I hear Mom grumbling. "Why doesn't he come to the door like usual?" She looks out the window.

"Too cold out," I say, grabbing my coat.

"That's never stopped him before. . . ." She eyes my outfit. "But you're not too worried about that, I suppose."

I zip up my spiky, low-heeled boots. "Heated house to heated car."

"Where are you two going?" She folds her arms across her chest and leans against the wall, watching me carefully.

I avoid eye contact. "We're staying at his place, watching videos."

"For his birthday?"

I roll my eyes. "It's what he wants."

"Then why the . . . outfit?"

"Because it's his *birthday*." As soon as I say it, I know it's not enough of an answer. "We might go for a bite to eat or something." Not entirely untrue.

"Is his mother home?"

"Yes." Also not entirely untrue—there is a framed eight-by-ten of her on the wall. I finish buttoning my coat. "Are we done with the inquisition?"

She gives me a long, hard stare. "Be home by eleven. It's a school night."

"Bye," I say, turning around and opening the door.

"Hey!" she says, pointing to her cheek.

I hesitate, then blow her a kiss and dash to Mike's car.

"I gotta start calling you an hour before I get here," he says as soon as I shut the door behind me.

As he backs out of the driveway, I reach for his hand. "Happy birthday to you," I sing cheerily.

He grins, looking at my outfit. "It sure is."

"What do you feel like watching?"

"A couple of guys from work wanted to meet me at Joe Junior's for a bite to eat."

"Do you want to go?"

He shrugs. "I told them we'd stop by."

"Oh. Why didn't you tell me?"

"Didn't think you'd mind." He looks at me. "*Do* you mind?"

"I guess not. It's your birthday."

Tonight is All-You-Can-Eat Wing Night, and Joe Junior's is packed. We squeeze through the throngs to a table of guys I don't know and their girlfriends. A few of the faces I recognize as guys who were in the same year as Mike at Melville.

My stomach flips as I realize one of them is Phil Taylor, older brother of Rick Taylor. *The same Rick Taylor who threw garbage at Uncle Sandeep's car this afternoon.* We're pointed toward two seats that were saved for us and I shrink into mine.

As I look around the table, I notice something I've never noticed before: I'm the only brown face there. There are no other, what Melville's principal refers to as, "minorities." In fact, as I look around the restaurant, I realize that there are only a handful of us in the entire place. *You could fit in and cloak your differences. . . .*

Throughout dinner, I hardly say a word. Mike and his buddies laugh and joke, over and around me, but I don't hear a word. I hear thuds against a car, words shot like bullets.

In this setting, I barely recognize Mike. He's so far away from the Mike I started dating last year. Suddenly I wonder if this part of Mike was always there and I just never saw it, never bothered to dig a little deeper, like with Mom and her family.

As we finish dinner, Mike jabs me in the ribs. "What's up?" he asks.

I shrug. "Nothing."

Outside, he gives his friends one-armed guy-hugs and we walk a block to the car. He starts it up, turns on the heat, and rubs his hands together. I huddle in the passenger seat, pulling my coat up around my neck.

"You sure nothing's up?" he says, blowing on his hands.

I hesitate for a moment, then look at him. "I wish you had told me we were coming to Joe Junior's."

He turns on the radio. "It was a last-minute thing, and I didn't think it was a big deal."

"Yeah, but . . . I thought we were going to have a nice, quiet evening. That's what you said you wanted."

He gives me an apologetic look. "The guys asked me and it sounded like fun." He puts his hand on the back of my neck and pulls me toward him. "We could still have that quiet evening."

He threads his fingers through my hair, kissing me long and soft on the mouth. His hands are warm, and I feel his body heat through our coats. My head starts swimming. Everything that happened today dissipates. He moves to my ear, then kisses my neck—his lips are soft and gentle, like fingertips on a floor, searching for shards of broken glass. I feel drugged. I open my eyes a little and the bright, neon green Joe Junior's sign in the distance comes into focus.

I pull back. "No."

He massages the base of my neck. "Right. Let's go somewhere else."

I pull away from his hand. "No, Mike."

He sits back in his seat. "What's the matter?"

"I had a really bad day," I say, leaning against the passenger door. He raises his eyebrows but says nothing. "I had a fight with Molly, and Uncle Sandeep—"

He looks out the window and mumbles, "Sounds like he's been a royal pain in the ass since he came around."

My voice goes up an octave. "I never said that! And no, he's not a pain in the anything. He's my *uncle*. Part of my family. What if one of your mom's brothers came back after fifteen years? Wouldn't you want to know something about him?"

"Wouldn't happen to my mom. All her loser brothers live five minutes away." He fiddles with the heat knobs. "Your family is your mom, Sammy. This guy doesn't know you from a hole in the wall. What does he want? Why'd he come around now, anyway?"

"Because he's family and because me and my mom are important to him!"

"What—he just figured that out?"

Okay, birthday or not, I've had enough. "Didn't you say that what happened on September eleventh made you see how important your mom is to you?"

He drops his head to one side and looks out the window.

I lean forward so that I can see his eyes. "Mike? A bunch of guys threw cans and garbage at Uncle Sandeep's car today."

He turns back to examine the steering wheel. "Did he tell you that?"

"Molly and I were in the car with him!"

He jerks his head around, eyes full of concern. "Did anything happen to you?"

I shake my head. "I'm not hurt, if that's what you mean."

He reaches out to stroke my earlobe.

"Mike, they said horrible things, and one of the guys was *Rick Taylor.*"

I wait for him to say something, to express shock, or horror. But several moments pass and he stays quiet. "Mike?" I say, leaning forward to look at his face.

"Look, I'm not saying what they did was right, Sam." He turns to face me. "But maybe if you didn't hang out with your uncle so much, you wouldn't have to deal with that kind of crap."

I'm stunned. Words slip through my teeth like smoke. I can't look at him. If I do, I might burst into tears.

"You could pass for anything. When I first met you, I thought you were Mexican."

My voice comes out as a gravelly whisper. "But I'm not. I'm Indian-American just like my mom . . . and Sikh, like my uncle."

He turns the music up, and the lyrics of *Get Rich or Die Tryin'* fill the little black Civic. "Who has to know?" he says.

I look out the window on my side.

Me. I know.

Although he enfolds my hand in his, the drive home is quiet and stiff. When he stops, I give him a halfhearted kiss and scramble out. The night did not go as smoothly as I had hoped. Not even close. But then, lately, nothing has been going very smoothly.

Chapter 6

First-period calculus drones on with Mr. Lim's back to the class. His entire body jiggles as he makes endless tables and symbols on the board. Lim's class offers a bit of relief from the constant barrage of September eleventh hyperawareness. It's the only class where we don't have to talk about the attacks. In here it's just numbers and formulas; things that make sense and have answers you can prove.

Lim and my mom seem to be the only people trying to *avoid* all the mass media coverage of what happened. When I leave my house, it's everywhere, all the time. Not that Mom doesn't talk about it or think about it. I know she does. It's in the little comments she makes about "our world these days," and the looks she darts out the window whenever there's a loud noise. She's taking the whole "don't let them win" thing to heart. Only it's a lot harder to do when things like what happened yesterday happen.

I haven't seen Molly yet, but she left three messages for me last night on my cell:

—*"Hi, Sammy. That was something this afternoon—I'm still reeling! Call me back."*

—*"Sam, I know you're out with Mike, but I just wanted to see how you're doing. I can't get it all out of my head! We've known those guys forever, why would they do something like that? Call me!"*

—*"Me again. Last call, I promise. I'm still shook up, but I just remembered you're out for birthday fun. If you do anything interesting, I want a detailed report. Meet me at my locker before class starts?"*

I never called her back and didn't meet her this morning.

Somehow, without my okay, everything has changed—overnight. I can't pinpoint what the change is, or exactly when it happened, but *nothing* is the same.

A movement in the hallway catches my eye. I turn to see Molly waving frantically, just behind the door. I look at Lim, who still has his back turned. I clear my throat loudly and scrape my chair against the floor.

Lim turns around. "Yes, Ms. All-oo-ali?"

"Can I use the bathroom, please?"

"I'm sure you *can*, but yes, you *may*. Next time, please go before class."

I catch up with Molly down the hall.

"Didn't you get my messages?" she asks, as soon as we're away from any open classroom doors.

I nod. "I got home late."

"Why didn't you meet me at my locker?"

"Got in late today." Not entirely untrue. I was definitely later than early.

She grabs my elbow. "Sammy, I can't get what happened yesterday out of my head!"

You can't get it out of your head?

"You must be totally *freaking*. What about Uncle Sandeep? Is he okay?"

"I haven't talked to him yet. Went out with Mike last night, remember?"

She throws her head back. "Oh crud, yeah." She looks at me, eyes widening. "Did you . . ."

"After the afternoon we had?"

She shrugs. "Comfort . . . ?"

"Hardly. Let's just say it didn't go very well."

Her mouth drops open. "Why not?"

I grip a lock on a locker and give it a tug. "We had dinner with Rick Taylor's brother."

Her eyes grow twice their usual size. "Who? *Why?*"

I shake my head slowly. "He and Mike were in the same year, and they had the same classes together."

Her saucer eyes narrow into buttonholes. "Did you tell Mike what Rick did?"

I nod.

She leans forward. "Aaaand?"

I shrug. "And nothing." I take a breath before my voice cracks.

She strokes my arm. "Don't worry, Sam. Between me and your uncle, we'll make sure you never walk home alone."

"I'm not worried." I look at the floor. "What about Bobbi?"

She stops stroking and leans against the wall of lockers. "Bobbi's not as bad as we thought she was, Sam."

"Come on, Moll. She drives a pink Lexus to school."

She giggles. "I know, but once you get past that, and the clothes, shoes, parties, and oodles of money . . . she's not so bad."

I roll my eyes. "Yeah."

We start walking. "Meet me at my locker after school?" she whispers as she rounds the bend to her class. I feel pinpricks behind my eyes. My world is still spinning away, but at least Molly's back.

I nod and slip quietly back into calculus. The clock shows twenty minutes since I left, but Lim has had his back turned the whole time, and most of the back row is asleep. I pray that my osmosis method of learning kicks into overdrive for this class.

The rest of the day is like a movie montage. I catch Balvir in the smokers' corner with a couple of other Indian girls in similar dress. I wonder why I've never focused in on them before? I would always walk by and register a brown mini-mob, but never stopped to look at any faces. Sometimes I think I just walked by and didn't even notice they were there at all. Funny what makes it onto your radar and what blips off the screen.

Rick Taylor, Chuck Banfield, and Simon Monroe lurk in a nearby corner. I've spent the last ten years avoiding those guys, and now they're everywhere. My stomach lurches at the very thought of them. When I see them, I have to lean against a wall for a moment to calm my stomach.

Bobbi Lewis floats by occasionally, all caramel and gold and bronze and pink. People I know wave and greet me in the halls. I wave and nod, feeling like a satellite, floating above it all.

In Ms. Lesiak's English class, we put the healthy discussion of the Trade Center attacks on hold while she gives us a lesson on the proper uses of a comma. Thank God for small favors. I still don't know what I'm going to write about.

Since my lunch is fourth period and Molly's is third, I usually try to get homework done during that time. Today I stare at a blank page for fifty minutes while snippets from yesterday's ride home play an endless loop in my brain. *Thud! Crash! Go back home, Osama!*

I pull out my cell phone and dial Uncle Sandeep. He did say I could call him anytime.

He answers halfway through the first ring. "Samar?"

"Hi, Uncle Sandeep."

"What is it? Are you all right?"

I stifle a sob. "I feel . . . I don't know . . ."

"Shall I come to get you? Are you finished at school?"

I almost come apart at the sound of genuine concern and caring in his voice. One . . . two . . . three, breathe. "No. I still have a couple of classes left."

"Shall I pick you up after school?"

"Yes," I say, barely above a whisper.

The rest of the afternoon passes in exactly the same way as the morning. After my last class, I rush outside.

Uncle Sandeep's car is out front and waiting. "Shall we drive and see where we end up?"

I nod and buckle my seatbelt. He drives out onto the main street, taking the ramp to the highway.

"Um, as long as we don't go out of state," I say.

He laughs. "I'm glad you still have your sense of humor!"

"Hasn't been easy."

His smile fades. "I'm sorry you had to go through that with me, Samar."

"It sort of brought me back in time, you know?"

He shakes his head. "No, tell me."

"I went through stuff like that—not as bad as *that*, but sort of the same kind of thing—when I was a kid."

He nods. "Of course."

I turn to him. "See? You say, 'of course,' but it's never been something I could talk easily with Mom about."

He knits his brow. "Why not? Sharan would understand."

"I don't know. She always drove home the point that I'm no different from anyone else . . . and that I should 'excel and surpass' everyone around me . . . like that would be my protection."

He makes a *tsk* sound with his teeth and tongue like Mom does. "She didn't want you to grow up feeling different, Samar—like she did."

"And I didn't, really . . . other than those few incidents, which I basically put out of my mind until . . . until the other day. But now," I continue, "I couldn't feel *more* different. I feel like the *epitome* of different—from everyone. I feel like there's no one else like me on this whole planet."

He nods, still saying nothing. His silence is a fill-in-the-blank, and my mouth suddenly feels like a leaky, overflowing pen. "It's like when I was a kid—I'd be happily joining in the fun on the playground, and then one of the girls would say something to me like, 'There are no dark people in Cinderella, so you can't play.'"

He turns into the parking lot of a large white building and brings the car to a stop. "I'm sorry, Samar. In some ways, I feel responsible for bringing this into you and your mother's lives again."

"But you also brought important information . . . information that Mom never gave me."

He lets out a sigh. "Whether or not that's positive is up for debate, if you ask your mother."

"It's positive for *me*," I say vehemently. "I had no idea how much I don't know! I get straight As at school, but if you ask me anything about who I am and where I come from, I might as well tattoo the word 'clueless' on my forehead." I look at my lap. "And you know what? It never mattered as much before . . . before you came around."

He leans across to squeeze me in a one-armed hug, our cheeks smushing together. Then he pauses before looking out the window. "I had no idea we would end up here," he says softly. "But now that we are, it seems the perfect place to be. Would you like to come inside with me?"

"Where are we?" I say, suddenly noticing our surroundings. I peer out the windshield. But before he says a single word, I have a funny feeling I already know.

The squiggly character above the double doors is the same one on the website that crashed my computer. The words above the character read EK ONKAR, and the line above that, ONE UNIVERSAL CREATOR.

"This is the *gurdwara*, the temple, I attend. I come here because they do the service in English as well as Punjabi. I like to know how to translate the scriptures so that I can share them with others who perhaps don't speak or understand the language." He looks at me. "It's a Friday afternoon, so it'll be nearly empty. . . ."

I stay glued to my seat, staring uncertainly at the building. It looks a bit cold, uninviting. Or is that how Mom described temples she went to as a child?

"If you don't want to, it's fine . . . we can keep driving," he says gently.

I imagine the scene when Mom finds out. I'm accustomed to doing things behind her back, but drinking a beer, experimenting with smoking, and making out with Mike are not the same as this. This is religion—Mom's blastoff point. This, and her parents. Here I am with her brother, who she just fought with, about to go into a Sikh temple. But I know it's something I need to do. I take a deep breath and nod.

Uncle Sandeep gives me an "are you sure?" look, then climbs out. I open the door with trembly fingers and follow him into the building.

The first thing I notice is the smell. Onions, incense, butter, old carpeting. Then I notice the space. Lots and lots of space. The ceilings are high, and it feels much bigger than it looks from the outside.

There are rows and rows of small, square cubbyholes to the right along the length of the wall, like the cubbies I had in kindergarten. Some of them have pairs of shoes in them. Uncle Sandeep takes his boots off and places them in one of the little cubbyholes. He tells me to do the same.

At first I panic, because I'm wearing lumpy socks, one with a hole where my big toe pokes out and the other where my pinky toe pokes out. I wonder if I should tell him, in case that's offensive. Maybe I should go sit in the car until he's done. . . .

But he ushers me on. He explains quietly that no one is allowed into the prayer area with their shoes on because it's a sign of disrespect to traipse into sacred space with dirty shoes and that in some temples in India, you're required to wash your feet before going in. All of a sudden, it makes sense why Mom makes everyone take their shoes off when they come into our house. Who knew that coming to a place she detests would give me an insight into my own mother?

Next to the stairs, leading into the main prayer room, is a large cardboard box with brightly colored scarves and pieces of cloth. Uncle Sandeep pulls out an eggplant-colored one and ties it around my head.

"You must cover your head, Samar. It's another way to show respect and humility in the Gurus' house."

I'm not sure I should have agreed to come in. I feel more out of place in here than I did in church with Molly. At least there, I *knew* I didn't belong. I knew, and everyone else knew, that I was just passing through, a visitor. Here, I feel like I should know all this stuff. Besides which, Uncle Sandeep seems to have transformed into a somber and very serious man who gives instructions on how to be respectful and humble.

Maybe Mike was right. I know nothing about this man. Maybe Mom was right—maybe these people want to turn me into a rule-following, silent, hair-growing, "good" girl. I take a step back. I want to tell Uncle Sandeep I've changed my mind and I'd like to go home now. I think about pulling out my cell phone and calling Mom.

Before I can do anything, Uncle Sandeep takes my arm. He leads me to a very old woman dressed completely in white. Her hair is pulled back into a satiny white bun and covered with a long, translucent white scarf. Uncle Sandeep says something to her in Punjabi. She looks at me and smiles a deeply creased smile, illuminating her skin, which is the exact color of the young gingerroot Mom uses in her noodle dishes. The old woman takes my hand firmly in hers.

"Go with Bibi-ji," he says.

"Where are you going?" I whisper as loudly as possible without screaming.

"I'll be directly ahead of you. You'll see me at all times, I promise. Men and women do not sit together in a gurdwara. You will be fine, trust me."

The old woman has a grip on my hand stronger than Mike's, and she leads me up the stairs. I follow, feeling powerless and pissed off and freaked out all at once.

We walk into a huge, brightly lit room. There are framed posters of turbaned, bearded men on the walls, and a canopy at the far end of the room with a big book underneath it—the Guru Granth Sahib, the holy book I read about on one of the websites. Sitting behind the book is an old man with a white turban, white clothes, and a white beard and mustache. He waves what looks like the Olympic torch—except instead of the flame, there's long white hair coming out of it—back and forth over the book. Next to the canopy is an empty, low stage with microphones and drums and other instruments. Strung around each window and the top of the canopy are multicolored Christmas lights.

Uncle Sandeep is ahead of the old woman, who pulls me along. He stops briefly, just after we get into the room, and slips me a five-dollar bill. I stare at it in my hand until the old woman looks at me, smiles encouragingly, and tugs me forward.

Uncle Sandeep walks up the center of the room, drops a bill into a box set up in front of the holy book, the Guru Granth Sahib, and kneels down to touch his forehead to the ground. Then he walks clear across the room to sit down.

The old woman does the same and indicates that I should follow. I drop my bill—first, way before the box and then, when I pick it up to try again, way behind it. The old woman shakes her head and motions for me to come to her side. She walks away from where Uncle Sandeep is sitting and sits at the extreme opposite end of the room. She motions for me to sit cross-legged like Uncle Sandeep, though she's having trouble doing that herself. She finally folds her legs at her side and leans on one hand.

I look at Uncle Sandeep across the room. He's sitting near a couple of other turbaned guys, one older with a graying beard and mustache, and the other younger like Uncle Sandeep, but a lot thinner and taller. Uncle Sandeep has his eyes closed and looks like he's muttering to himself.

I look out of the corner of my eye at the old woman next to me. We're the only two on the "women's side." She has a round face with permanent smile lines. Everything about her is round: huge, heaving breasts, a belly like a cloud on her lap, and toes and fingers that are plump and oiled. She smells like the cardamom and clarified butter that Mom sometimes uses in her cooking.

There's something about this woman that draws me completely into what feels like an invisible hug. Her eyes are closed, and she rocks back and forth to the chanting of the man in the front of the room holding the white-haired torch. Everyone seems to be in their own space. Like when I zone out during lunch period, or during tests. Not a bad idea right now, I suppose. I close my eyes.

Little by little, a kind of quiet seeps into me, like a stain spreading on a paper towel. Uncle Sandeep, the old woman,

Molly, Mom, Rick Taylor, Chuck Banfield, Simon Monroe, Mike, Bobbi Lewis, Balvir, tests, school . . . they all fall away.

I hear the whirr of the ceiling fan above me and the breathing of the old woman next to me. I begin to rock, even before I realize I'm doing it. The man reading the words at the front of the room recites them first in Punjabi, then the same line again in English. He seems to have done this so often that everything flows together, almost into one long sentence. His voice rises and falls in a gentle pulse. I tune into that—the rhythm, zeroing in on the English words.

"*One universal creator God . . . the name is Truth . . . Creative Being personified . . . No fear, no hatred . . .*"

Bit by bit, the reverence and the lulling words snake their way through my ears, settling like a mist somewhere deep inside me—in a place where other words have left festering, bubbling wounds. I begin to *see* what's behind my eyes so clearly and vividly, I feel I could reach out and touch it.

I see a long line of people, stretching far back into an endless horizon. People from way back in time. Mom's people and, I guess, my dad's people. A jolt zings through my body. *My* people. A sea of faces I don't recognize.

". . . *the undying, beyond birth . . . self-sustaining . . . Truth in the primal beginning, Truth throughout the ages . . . Truth here and now . . .*"

I see myself as one small point in this long, long chain of people who stretch way out to infinity. And it hits me. I wouldn't, *couldn't*, be here if any one of those people hadn't survived many of the tragedies we discussed in history class—

holocausts, natural disasters, diseases, wars, famines . . .

The thought of that is so astounding that my eyes fly open and I let out a gasp. The old woman turns to me and kindly motions for me to be quiet. I close my eyes again, eager to get that feeling and image back. But it's gone. Instead I see all these layers. Like rings on a tree trunk, or the layers of the earth's crust that Ms. Ortiz showed us in geography last year. "Each layer is stronger when the one beneath it is solid," she had said.

"Oh Great Creator, how can we become pure and truthful, honest and innocent . . . and break free of the illusion?"

It dawns on me, clear as a summer sky, how wrapping a turban, speaking the language of your parents' parents' parents, and celebrating the same holidays that everyone before you celebrated are all like little thank-yous to those who survived. Those seemingly small things are a long-held memory whispered from the lips of the past into the ear of the future.

Remembering. It's all about remembering.

Suddenly, what feels like a raging fire begins at the bottom of my spine. Why has Mom kept all this from me? She had no right! I've always had what Molly has, and my own *mother* kept me from it. A tremor from so far inside tears its way through the center of my body, and I feel as if I'll split in two.

A warm hand lands gently on my forearm. I shudder and my eyes snap open. The old woman gazes into my face. *"Bas,"* she says, motioning for me to stand. *"Chalo."*

I see that Uncle Sandeep is standing too. I rise slowly, blood pumping furiously in my temples, and follow the woman stiffly.

When we get back to the shoe cubbies, Uncle Sandeep smiles, his eyes looking relaxed. "I saw you with the peace," he says.

I shake my head. My throat is tight, and my voice comes out as a cross between a croak and a squeal. "A piece of what?" I ask, feeling disoriented and aflame all at once.

He shakes his head. "The peace, *peace*," he says, exasperated. "The peace in your heart. That's the whole reason I come here, and why I wanted to bring you here."

I look sharply into his eyes. "You knew all along we were coming here?"

He shrugs as we head out the door. "No. Not consciously. I knew that I wanted to bring you *someday* . . . we just ended up here today." I give him a long, hard look before we get into the car, but he becomes absorbed in a spot on his shirtsleeve.

He throws the car into reverse. "I wish we could have stayed for the *langar*—it's a communal meal that anyone is welcome to after each service. That's an integral part of Sikhism, you know, the belief that everyone is entitled to food and shelter. That's why all gurdwaras are open to anyone who needs those things. . . ."

I tune him out as I try to hang on to the feelings and images I had inside the gurdwara. I look out the windshield, and for the first time, I notice the American flag blowing in the wind along with the other flags above the building. As we make our way through the streets on our way to the expressway, I see that all the Indian shops and bodegas in the area have huge American flags draped across their display windows as well. We drive past a taxi stand where several cab drivers sit, waiting for fares. Some wear turbans like Uncle Sandeep. They sip their hot drinks or doze inside their cars. All of them have PROUD TO BE AN AMERICAN stickers displayed prominently in their windshields.

I suddenly feel like I've entered a bizarre parallel universe where everything is flipped around and makes no sense whatsoever—like all things American and all things Indian were thrown up in the air and landed back in all the wrong places, just to confuse the hell out of me.

I flip open my cell phone as Uncle Sandeep pulls onto the expressway. Twelve messages and seven missed calls.

Chapter 7

All the lights are on, and the house seems alive from the outside, buzzing with Mom's frenetic energy. As Uncle Sandeep pulls into the driveway, the front door flies open and Mom comes rushing out in her slippers. "Sammy, my baby! Are you all right, sweetheart?"

Her face is splotchy and her eyes are full of red veins. She has a bunch of tissues in one hand. As soon as I climb out of the car, she envelops me in a crushing hold. After a moment, she pushes me out for an inspection.

"What happened? Are you hurt? Isn't your cell phone working? I left several messages! Where did you find her, Sandeep?"

God. I should have expected her usual overreaction to me being the teensiest bit late. "I'm fine," I say, wriggling out of her arms. I walk past her and into the house.

"Sammy, Sandeep . . . will someone please tell me what is going on?"

Uncle Sandeep takes off his boots, but leaves his coat, scarf, and gloves on. Smart guy. The tension between him and Mom might be temporarily suspended because she's been frantic about me, but Mom never forgets.

He sits in a chair at the kitchen table and motions for me to sit next to him. Then he turns to Mom. "Sharan, sit down."

Her face drains of color. "It's that bad?" she whispers, sinking into a nearby chair. She looks at me. "Why didn't you come to me, Sammy?"

She reaches for my hand, and I snatch it away. I say nothing. I can't even look at her.

"Samar, tell me what is going on here," she demands, her voice rising.

Uncle Sandeep says softly, "Samar is fine. She has not been harmed in any way. Really, Sharan—she's fine. She called me because she was upset, and we went for a drive. That's all."

Mom sighs, her shoulders sagging in relief. But only for a moment. Then she sits up straight, color popping back up into her neck and face. "My God, Sammy, do you know what you put me through? Molly called here looking for you when you didn't meet her after school like you had agreed. . . ."

Oh my God, *Molly!* I had completely forgotten I was supposed to meet her at her locker!

"When an hour passed and then another and another, we both became hysterical! After the incident the other day, and you not showing up to meet Molly, I—my imagination ran wild with what might be happening!" She stands up and begins pacing. "Sammy, I raised you better than this. You should know better than to disappear off the face of the earth without so much as a phone call, not even to your best friend!" She puts her hands on her hips. "And a four-hour drive? Where on earth did you two go?"

Uncle Sandeep looks at me.

For the first time all evening, I look directly at Mom. My eyes narrow slightly and my body is rigid, but my voice stays calm. "We were gone only about three hours, and Uncle Sandeep and I went to a gurdwara."

Mom's hand flutters to her cheek as if she's just been slapped. She looks at Uncle Sandeep. "She went *where*?"

He shifts in his seat. "Sharan, I picked her up after classes—I had no idea she was supposed to meet Molly. . . ."

"And you ended up in a *gurdwara*, of all places?"

His voice is calm, like a horse-whisperer soothing a wild stallion. "I didn't drag her there, Sharan. She had a choice."

"I *wanted* to go," I say. My stomach churns the way it does every time I'm about to face off with Mom.

Her face blanches. "You *wanted* to go?" She turns to Uncle Sandeep. "You shouldn't have done this, Sandeep. . . . These are the things that turn daughters against their mothers. . . ." Tears shine in the corners of her eyes. She brushes them away with her shaky fingertips.

My hard shell crumbles like parched earth. Just who is the wounded victim here, anyway? I stand up, my voice choking out. "No, *you* turned me against you! Uncle Sandeep only tried to help! But you don't want him around me either, do you? Just like your parents and every other family member—you don't want *anyone* around me!" Hot tears gush down my cheeks and neck. My fists clench and unclench at my sides.

"Are you afraid I might like them better than you? 'Cause you're probably right! The only way you can keep anyone around is to keep them away from everyone else! That's probably what you did to Dad—suffocated him till he couldn't stand you anymore, just like you're suffocating me—"

SMACK!

I reel back and fall into the chair behind me.

"Sharan!" Uncle Sandeep is at my side in an instant.

Mom staggers back into a chair, looking at her hand with a "what have you done?" expression, as if it just grew a separate brain. I stare at her through a curtain of wavy hair and reach up to touch my cheek. My mother has never before laid a hand on me.

She leans forward, reaching for my face. "Sammy, I . . ."

Something slow and ugly—something I never knew was there—rumbles up from deep inside. I sharpen my words like daggers and throw them with noxious precision. "I wish . . . that *you* were the one who left . . . instead of Dad."

Then I run upstairs to my bedroom, before drowning in another flood of tears.

Saturday morning I sleep late. When I finally roll out of bed, it's almost eleven. I throw the covers back and quickly get dressed. I've got to get out of the house before Mom's done with her Saturday morning clients. Staying here all day in the same house with her is *not* an option. I call Molly to let her know I'm coming, stuff my homework and some clothes into my backpack, and run out the door.

The sound of Mom's hand connecting with my face resonates in my head the whole five blocks to Molly's house. I reach up to stroke my cheek. Mom doesn't give a damn about me! It's all about *her* and how much *she* doesn't want to see her parents, and how my father's family was mean to *her*. What about me?

Mom always said, "Let your own truth be your guiding light, even if it's not the same as anyone else's." It never occurred to me that that might include her. Why didn't I think to find my own truth, even if it's not the same as Mom's?

"I've decided I'm moving out," I say when Molly answers the door. She steps aside and yanks me in.

"Good morning, Sammy!" her mother calls from the kitchen as Molly drags me up the stairs.

"Morning, Mrs. Mac!" I yell back.

"What's going on?" Molly asks as she shuts the bedroom door firmly behind her. "Why weren't you answering your cell? Your mom called me a million times looking for you last night! I was freaking out—you were supposed to meet me at my locker!"

I drop my backpack on her floor and fall back onto her bed. "Sorry, Moll. I just didn't want to deal with anyone last night." I cover my eyes with my forearm.

She looks a little hurt, but recovers quickly. "So what happened? I tried to call Mike's cell phone, but it kept going straight through to voice mail. . . . I didn't know if I should cover for you, or call the cops! Thank God your mom finally called and said that you were home safe. But she didn't sound too happy about it."

"She *smacked* me." I sit up as if it had just happened.

She gasps and lands hard on the bed next to me. "*Your* mom? Smacked you how? Like a little pat, or a flick? 'Cause I get that all the time. . . ."

"Like a smack on the face. Like in the movies when someone's delirious."

"*Were* you delirious?"

I lie back again and stare at the ceiling fan. "I've never been more clear in my life. I hate her, Moll. She ran my dad off, then my grandparents, and now she wants to run Uncle Sandeep off too. She wants me to have nobody but *her*."

Molly shakes her head, her hand covering her mouth. "You don't hate her, you're just mad. But God, I can't believe she smacked you. . . . I just can't picture her doing that! Was it like a hard slap?"

"It was a hard slap."

"What was she so mad about?" Then she jerks her head around. "Wait, did you say she ran your *dad* off?"

I nod.

"Since when do you use that word for that guy?"

"He was probably great, Moll! My mom's delusional. She said Uncle Sandeep was a slimeball too."

She gives me a look. "She did not say that, Sam."

"She might as well have! Whenever she talked about her parents, she said they were controlling and critical and miserable, and 'oppressive.' They're probably the nicest people in the world! I just can't believe I never tried to find out what they're like for myself, instead of believing her *lies*."

"'Cause they might not be lies," she says, cocking her head to one side. She slowly traces a pattern on the mattress between us. "It's never too late, you know . . . to find out for yourself, that is."

I sit up again. "I already thought about that. I thought maybe Uncle Sandeep and I could work on Mom . . . you know, maybe get her to agree to letting me see my grandparents." I hunch my shoulders and cross my arms. "But after yesterday, I can see that's impossible."

"You still haven't told me what exactly happened."

"Uncle Sandeep took me to a gurdwara—a Sikh temple."

Her eyes expand. "Whoa."

"Yeah. *Big* explosion."

She's quiet for a moment. Then she raises one apricot, barely there eyebrow. "So what're you gonna do?"

"I don't ever want to go back there."

"You're gonna have to go back. You can stay here for today, but my mom's not going to let you stay here if your mom's not cool with it."

I sigh. "I know. No wonder I never went against her! I have nowhere else to go! She really screwed things up for me."

"What about your uncle? Could you stay with him for a bit, until you clear your head?"

I shake my head. "It'll make things worse between him and Mom. He'll tell me to work it out with her first, I just know it."

"Hmm," she says, looking stumped.

I turn deliberately to look at her. "Maybe *you* could help me."

She looks at me suspiciously. "How?"

The wheels for Plan B start rumbling into motion. "Uncle Sandeep and I may not be able to convince Mom to let me see my grandparents . . ." I stand up and walk to Molly's dresser, my heart pumping with renewed zeal. "But you and I might be able to convince Uncle Sandeep to take me to see them . . . on his own! Mom doesn't have to know everything."

Her eyes widen, and she jumps up. "Ooooh, I love it."

"I'm going to meet my grandparents, Moll." I squeeze her hands and shiver.

Her eyes sparkle. "Even *I'm* getting butterflies in my belly."

I drop her hands and rummage through my backpack. "I'm going to call him right now."

"Now?"

"If he's free, we could meet him somewhere . . . at the mall, maybe. You did say you wanted to get your Christmas shopping done early this year, right?"

She grins and begins changing out of her sweats.

I flip open my cell phone and scroll through to Uncle Sandeep's number. My skin rises in goose bumps as I realize that a family Thanksgiving might actually be in the cards for me. With or without Mom.

After telling him that I have something urgent to discuss with him and it *has* to be in person, Uncle Sandeep agrees to meet me outside of Wok This Way in the food court of the mall. I leave out the part about Molly coming with me and us tag-teaming against him.

Molly and I get there early, grab some noodles and teriyaki chicken, and figure out our game plan. We know Uncle Sandeep wants me and my grandparents to meet, but we also know he would never go behind Mom's back to do it. So our strategy is to focus on the fact that I need to meet them no matter what, by any means necessary.

She leans forward. "Tell him it's your right to know your grandparents—no, wait, it's your *birthright.*"

"Ooh, that's good," I say, popping a piece of baby corn into my mouth. "I deserve to know them, and it's just plain wrong—no, *criminal*—to keep that from me!"

"Yes!" she says, pointing a chopstick at me.

I shovel a forkful of noodles into my mouth when I see Uncle Sandeep jog into the food court. He searches frantically around the tables. I wave, and he runs right over.

"Samar!" he says breathlessly. "What's wrong?"

"Um, nothing's wrong, exactly," I say, feeling bad that I worried him.

"What do you mean?" He wrinkles his brow and looks at Molly. "What's this about?"

She looks into her plate. So much for tag-teaming.

I straighten my spine and say, in my most serious and authoritative voice, "Uncle Sandeep, I have something very important to talk to you about."

He gives me a scolding look. "Does your mother know about this?"

I shake my head. "No, but—"

"Then this is wrong, Samar. Sharan is very upset that I took you to the gurdwara against her will, and rightly so! I never should have done so without her consent. This will only fuel her anger and mistrust."

"I want to talk to you about your parents," I say quickly, "my grandparents."

After a brief pause, his face softens. "What about them?"

Molly sets her chopsticks down and gives me an encouraging nod.

I look him in the eyes. "I want to meet them. I . . . I have a right to meet them."

"A *birthright*," Molly adds, coming back into the mix.

Uncle Sandeep looks from me to Molly and back again. With a sigh, he unravels his scarf, shrugs out of his coat, and sits down. "Okay, I'm listening," he says.

"All this time, Mom's had no contact with you and your parents. . . ."

"Which we respect," Molly throws in. "That's her choice."

I continue. "Yes, that's *her* choice—not necessarily mine. No one asked me what *I* wanted. Don't you think I deserve to know my own grandparents?"

He slouches in his seat. "Samar, this is something I've discussed at length with your mother. It's something she is dead set against."

I burst. "But isn't that unreasonable? I know you don't agree with her, Uncle Sandeep! You know it's totally unfair!"

He presses his lips together. "She is your mother, Samar," he says, shaking his head.

"This is crazy!" I shout, slamming my hand down on the

table. Several people at the next table turn around. I'm at once aware that we're the only table in the food court with a sweaty, anxious, turbaned guy having an impassioned meeting with someone pounding their fist on the table.

"Yes?" Molly says, leaning toward the people who are still staring. They turn back around, muttering to one another.

I lower my voice. "Don't they want to see me?" My chin begins to quiver. "How could they let her get away with this? Don't they care about meeting their only grandchild?"

He covers my hand with his. "Of course they do! Samar, you have no idea how much they long to see you. For years they've lived to catch snippets about you from cousins and friends who've happened to run into Sharan!"

My stomach flips. What kind of a mother would do something like this to her own child? Two thin streams meander down my cheeks. "Uncle Sandeep," I whisper, "if we leave it to Mom, I'll *never* get to know them."

Molly strokes my upper arm deliberately. "My grands are such a huge part of my life," she says, looking at Uncle Sandeep. "I can't imagine never knowing them."

Uncle Sandeep leans back in his chair, throws his head back, and rests his fists against his closed eyelids. When he sits forward again, he leans on one elbow, lets his breath out in a whoosh, and slides a finger under his turban to scratch his head.

"This is probably the biggest mistake I'll ever make—"

Before he can finish, I'm out of my seat, wrapping my arms around his neck.

"Yesss! Thank you, Uncle Sandeep—it's not a mistake, you'll see!" I grab a napkin off the table and blow my nose.

Molly's grinning from ear to ear. "So when'll it be?"

"Thanksgiving weekend!" I say.

Chapter 8

The few conversations I've had with Mike have been awkward. The last one went like this:

Me: I got a B+ on my last calc quiz.

Him: Cool.

Us: *silence.*

Him: Hey, 'member that guy Al I told you about, that works with me?

Me: Um, the one with the kid on the way?

Him: No—who has a kid on the way?

Me: I don't know, I thought you said someone had a kid on the way.

Him: No.

Me: Oh.

Us: *silence.*

Him: Anyway, Al got laid off last Friday. Can you believe that? Right before the holiday.

Me: Wow.

Us: *silence.*

Him: You hangin' with your mom for Thanksgiving?

Me: Uh, yeah.

I'm not telling him what I'm really doing. Based on the last time I saw him, I get the feeling he won't be as excited as I'd like him to be. He definitely won't be as excited as me and Molly.

Even though Molly always invites me to join her family for Thanksgiving, I don't like to leave Mom alone during major holidays. Not that she has ever said anything to me about it, and I know she would probably be fine, but I still feel bad leaving her all alone when the rest of the world is spending time with their families.

Usually Thanksgiving weekend is a holiday Mom and I celebrate by sleeping in, eating out or ordering in (if Mom's not inspired to make her Thanksgiving Cornish hen recipe), and catching up on homework for me and client reports for her. Then, if Molly's in town and not at some out-of-state family gathering, Mom tries to wrangle me and Molly into volunteering with Mom and her friends at some homeless shelter or women's place.

Except this time. This time I have a chance to spend a huge, family-oriented holiday with my own family. Sure, my mom is family too . . . but I mean a whole *bigger* family. A *real* family, with grandparents and an uncle and a big meal and laughter and conversation around clinking dinnerware—everything I've seen on TV shows and at Molly's house.

Ignoring a few twinges of guilt, I tell Mom I'll be driving to Pennadunkit Canyon for Thanksgiving weekend with Molly and a couple of friends. Since Molly's family will be gathered at her Great-Aunt Maggie's estate, no one will answer if Mom calls the house, and she won't ask how it was if she happens to run into Mrs. Mac sometime down the road. Plus, Molly said she'll cover if Mom calls her cell.

After apologizing for the thirty-ninth time for slapping me, Mom almost keels over in relief when I tell her where I'm going, so she doesn't interrogate me as much as she normally would.

For the next few days there's a little party going on in my chest. Each day that brings me closer to the weekend I'm to meet my grandparents and finally look into my history and my past feels like a little secret I guard and cherish.

But the days pass ever so achingly slowly. By the time we crawl into the second week of November, the little party in my chest has become a loud, thrashing concert in my stomach.

Ms. Lesiak calls me up after English class on Tuesday morning. "Samar, I noticed that you haven't submitted your paper."

I mumble something about being sorry and stressed, and that I'll get it to her as soon as possible.

She nods. "It's a difficult subject, I know," she says, "but I'm only asking for your thoughts and feelings. There is no wrong way to do this assignment, Samar. Why don't you get together with some of the other students to discuss it? Perhaps that will generate your own thoughts for the paper."

Wonderful, more Healthy Discussion and Debate.

"Sure," I say.

"I'll give you until after the holiday to get the paper back to me," she says. "After that, I deduct a letter grade for each day it's late."

"A whole letter grade?!"

"I'm sorry, Samar, but you're already a week late. I'm being very generous here."

I nod and walk out. I'm not one to put things off, but every time I start this paper, I zone out.

As I walk to lunch, Balvir falls into step beside me. "Hey, I heard your convo with Lesiak. Didn't mean to listen in, but I was getting my stuff."

"Yeah . . . sucks."

"Do you want to have lunch together? Maybe we could talk, like she said, and maybe it'll help you jump-start your paper."

I'm about to say, "No, thank you," when Lesiak's warning pops into my head: *I deduct a letter grade for each day it's late.*

"Yeah, all right."

She laughs. "Don't sound so excited!"

"Sorry, it's not personal."

"No worries. I'm pretty thick-skinned. Should we sit outside? It's a bit cold, but the sun's out. . . ."

I nod, and we head to a grassy spot off to one side of the field. We sit down, open our lunches, and begin eating in silence. On the field, several guys throw a football around during their gym period.

"I hate those guys," Balvir says, looking out at the field.

"All of them?" I ask, taking a bite from my sandwich.

She shakes her head. "No, just the one in the green, and that one . . . in the shorts."

I squint my eyes to see them better. The guys she's talking about are Chuck Banfield and Simon Monroe.

"They live on my street and have made life hell for us since we moved in."

I get a queasy feeling in my gut. "How?" I ask, but I think I already know.

"Oh . . . they throw things into our front yard, harass my sixty-year-old grandmother, chase my little brother home every night . . . I could go on."

We eat silently for a moment.

"They threw cans and garbage at my uncle's car," I say, looking out at the field. I feel her turning to look at me, then back out at the guys.

"Jackasses," she says. "Nothing else for their stunted brain cells to fixate on. Always picking on someone smaller or defenseless." And then she cups her hands around her mouth and yells, "You're SO big and strong!"

A couple of the guys turn to look at us with puzzled expressions. I want to blend into the tree. Chuck and Simon smirk and keep playing.

She turns to me with a triumphant smile. "I know they probably think I complimented them. Those lunkhead Neanderthals don't get subtlety or sarcasm. But it felt good to yell."

"They used to call me names and shove my face into the ground when I was a kid," I say quietly, the memory slithering back to the surface.

"I bet."

"I punched and scratched and yelled back, but . . ."

"But they traveled in clumps. And you were just you."

I nod and look at her. For a brief moment, our eyes meet. The flecks of yellow and gold in her liquid, cola-colored eyes are just like Mom's. I tumble into a moment in the past. A moment where I sat under a tree on the grass in the sun with Mom and told her about what was going on at school.

She gritted her teeth and pounded the ground. "Don't you let them make you believe you're less than, Sammy! You're every bit as good—better, even! You're smarter, lovelier . . ." Her eyes welled up and she cupped my face in her hands. "And kinder. You could run circles around them. Excel and surpass them, sweetheart . . . you'll be so far out of their league, they'll never be able to touch you again!"

Then she set me on the "math path." Every type of math book and game you could buy, she bought. For some reason, Mom thought math would be the liberating force in my life.

I look back at Balvir, then down at her kara bangle. An idea begins to take shape in my mind. After our trip to the gurdwara, Uncle Sandeep told me about the Five Ks of Sikhism: the kara bangle, symbolizing right thought and action; the kesh (unshorn hair), symbolizing God's wisdom; the kanga (comb), symbolizing cleanliness; the kachha (boxer shorts), symbolizing chastity and modesty; and the kirpan (ceremonial dagger), symbolizing readiness to defend one's honor and faith.

Balvir is Sikh, Indian, and Punjabi. The exact same equation as Mom, and her mom . . . and, I guess, me. Plus, she's my age. She might be able to offer me some insight into the experience that I can't get from anyone else.

"Hey," I begin. My tongue feels like a rock. "Could you recommend some good books or . . . something on Sikhism? Like for young people? Even if it's for older people, that's cool too. . . . I just want to learn a bit more about it."

She looks at me for a long moment, like a jeweler appraises gems for authenticity. I feel like I'm morphing into a giant coconut right there on the field, in front of her very eyes. Finally she looks up into the bare branches above us.

"Try SikhOut.org—smart people keepin' it real. Then, if you really feel ambitious, you could check out Sikhchic. com and SepiaMutiny.com. Those two are blogs, and"—she gives me a grin—"they might be a bit advanced for you right now."

I think about Mom and what she sometimes suggests to clients. "What about groups . . . or like a center for Sikh youth or something . . . ?"

"*Groups?*" She looks at me as if my ignorance is astonishing. I'm a coconut that has doubled in size.

"Girl, you need friends. *That's* your group. Find some Indian peeps to hang out with."

I shift my weight, suddenly feeling like I'm sitting on a hill of pebbles. I realize we haven't discussed anything about the paper I have due for Lesiak in about three weeks and am relieved at the opportunity to change the subject. "So, about Lesiak's assignment . . ."

She nods. "Yeah, I keep wondering what your thoughts are on that, but you never say anything in class."

"What did you write about?"

She squints at the sky. "I wrote about the internment camps during World War II, when there was mass paranoia about the Japanese, and I linked it to the mass hysteria and paranoia about Muslims after the attacks."

I stare at her.

She looks at me as if searching for something. She sighs and continues. "You do know about the internment camps, right? You know, when hundreds of thousands of Japanese and Japanese Americans were forcibly removed from their homes and sent off to 'camps' because the government thought they could be 'enemies of the state' or spies?"

I slowly shake my head, racking my brain for the American history lesson that would have taught us about this.

She laughs. "God, girl. Do you even know who you are? You need to learn about more than just your Sikhness; you need to learn about your American-ness, too! Look it up online when you're doing research for your paper. Check out Wikipedia— they have other links on there that you can follow."

I wonder why I always feel so dumb when I talk to Balvir. And I know that by asking my next question I'm about to sound just as dumb as I feel. "How do you know all this stuff?"

She stops laughing. "I do research. I dig. I ask questions. You learn from living with a family like mine that most of the time what people tell you and what's *true* are two different things. I want to find out for myself." She sighs again. "History is more than just a class at school, Sammy. What happened then could happen now, too."

I shake my head again. "What do you mean?"

She gives me a hard look. "The enemy during that war was anyone of Japanese ancestry."

I nod. "So . . . ?"

"Who's the enemy now?"

I wonder why she would ask the obvious. "Terrorists?"

"And what do they look like?"

Suddenly the breath is sucked out of my lungs. *Uncle Sandeep.*

"Aaaah! Mission control, we have contact! They look like you and me, Sammy. They look like my brother and my father and my uncles." She sits quietly next to me for a moment, as I struggle with that realization.

"But, but . . . you don't think they could . . . that they would . . ."

She shrugs. "Who knows?" Then she crumples up her brown paper bag and stands up. "C'mon," she says. "We have to get back."

That night I get to work on my paper. I start by going right to Wikipedia and typing in "Japanese internment camps." Wow. Balvir knows what she's talking about. Everything she said is true.

I follow link after link until my heart is pounding furiously in my ears. I stand up and pace back and forth in my room until I hear Mom in the kitchen, then sprint downstairs.

"Mom! Did you know about the Japanese internment camps during World War II?"

She stops running the water and turns to look at me. "A

little. It's something that affected a client I had some time back. Why? Are you doing research for school?"

"Do you think they could do that again? You know, round up people who look like 'terrorists' and send them to some kind of internment camp?"

Hearing the note of hysteria in my voice, she steps forward and holds me in one of her tight Mom-hugs; the ones she gives me when she's trying to wring all the panic out. "Who told you that?" she asks, leading me to the table and sitting down.

"A . . . a friend . . . at school."

She wrinkles her brow and stares down at the table for a moment. "Sammy, we're at a real turning point in the history of this nation. We've had an attack on American soil. . . ."

"But that's what happened during World War II! Pearl Harbor!"

She nods slowly. "Yes. There are similarities." She reaches for my hand, stroking the back of it slowly with her thumb. "But it doesn't help to become frantic, Sammy. We can't predict what's going to happen . . . fear isn't going to help us gain control over anything."

I swallow hard. Mom always resorts to therapy talk when she doesn't know what to say. I get the sinking feeling that she might be a little scared, too. I pull my hand from hers and push my chair back. "I'm going to go back to my paper."

She nods but doesn't move from her spot. "Don't spend too much time worrying about things that might never happen, Sammy."

As soon as I'm in my room, I dial Uncle Sandeep.

"Hello, Samar!"

"Uncle Sandeep, do you think they'll send people who look like terrorists to internment camps like they did with the Japanese in World War II?"

A long pause. I squeeze the phone even closer to my ear.

Finally, he says clearly, "No."

I exhale. There is certainty in his voice. No shadows or doubts. For the first time since my conversation with Balvir, the panic in my chest gives a little. "No?"

"No," he repeats.

I drop onto my bed. "Why not?"

"Because, Samar, people today would not stand for it. We have evolved since then."

"But why did people stand for it then?"

He takes a deep breath, and I picture him looking up at the ceiling like he does when he's putting sentences together in his mind. "Well, I suppose for the same reasons people stand for any kind of violation of human rights: fear, anger, suspicion . . . But Samar, you must understand that the government apologized for what happened with the Japanese. There were reparations—not enough, of course, because you can never make up for something like that in dollars, but it was an admission of wrongdoing. And that is *something*."

I think about that for a moment. "But so what? That doesn't guarantee that it won't happen again." The panic isn't completely gone, but my heart is no longer pounding in my ears.

"Of course not." His voice is gentle. "We never have those

kinds of guarantees, my dear. But we must have some faith in the evolution of humankind. There is more good out there than you've been led to believe . . . more people are searching for the truth and discovering major flaws in the way things have been set up in the world than ever before."

I get the feeling that he's not even talking to me anymore. He seems to be off on some sort of inner ride through his mind.

"Certainly, there are still incidents and pockets of hatred . . . but on the whole, there is a mass outcry and movement toward justice and peace everywhere; it's something you won't see on television and in most news stories—"

I jump in before he can begin again. "So you're pretty sure nothing like that will happen?"

"Hmm? Oh, yes, very sure. Call me an eternal optimist, but I believe that while we'll no doubt deal with incidents like the one in the car several weeks ago, something on the scale of internment camps for women, children, the elderly . . . I don't think it's likely."

I lean back against my pillows. "Okay. Thanks, Uncle Sandeep."

"Of course, but what brought this on?"

I heave a sigh. "I was talking to a girl, Balvir, at school today about a paper we have to write on the attacks in New York City. She wrote about the internment camps during World War II . . . like what if that kind of thing happened now."

"Balvir?" He sounds hopeful. "She's Indian?"

"Yeah."

"Fantastic! How is your paper coming along?"

"It's not."

He laughs. "Well, I guess you'd better get off the phone, then."

When I hang up, I feel calmer. Still thrown off by the little tidbit of history Balvir dropped on me, but not panicked like before. Why didn't we learn about this in American history class?

I think about Uncle Sandeep and how much of a mystery he and Mom's parents have been to me my whole life. How much more about American history don't I know? How much more about my own family history don't I know?

I jump off my bed and boot up the computer. I type "SikhOut.org" into my browser. The site is warm: burgundy, amber, and rust, with gold details. I click on the Members Forum and am directed to a page where I have to register. I make sure it's free and register under the user name JerseyCoconut.

Once I'm in, I'm amazed. You'd never know it was a Sikh site if it didn't say so at the top of the page. The posters use phrases like *cray-z*, *wat a hotT!*, and *the girl is tight*. There are lots of little things you can play with other members, too— you can have snowball fights and throw ninja stars. I don't know what I expected, maybe all religion, Sikh stuff. And that's there too, but there are all kinds of other topics, from Politics to Sexuality to Plastic Surgery. I scroll through the subject headings:

Help! My parents won't let me shave my armpits!

To the dork who thinks grlz shouldn't wear turbans

Sexing up before marriage?

Help! I have a Muslim boyfriend!

For some strange, unknown reason, I wonder what life might've been like for Mom if sites like this had been around when she was in high school. I push it aside. Who cares?

I click on *To the dork who thinks grlz shouldn't wear turbans.*

HardKaurGrl: *U R a total loozer. Why shouldn't grlz wear turbans? I've seen some American Sikh women wear them, and they look amazing.*

Reply from MasalaBabe: *I tried it once and my mother wuz OK w/it, but Dad told me take it off. NOW.*

Reply from KingSingh: *turbans r 4 guyz, man. get over it. u have ur chunni's. keep em on ur head.*

I move on to *My parents won't let me shave my armpits!*

PunjabiKuri: *I can't handle gym class! My parents won't let me shave my underarms and everyone makes fun of me. And they should! I stink! Then I have to pour perfume all over myself and I smell like a flower with B.O. Help!*

Reply from HarmindHammer: *my sister uses some kind of cream.*

Reply from JattiRules: *ya, i use Neet, or Nair. u could wax 2. they say we can't cut hair, they don't say nothing about waxing or Neet.*

Reply from KingSingh: *It's the same thing. God put each hair on your body for a reason. If you mess with it, you're spitting in the face of the Gurus.*

I notice that no one on the forum calls themselves Indian; they all refer to themselves as "South Asian." I look it up and discover that "South Asian" is a term used to refer to people in the "diaspora," which means any place outside of the mother country that people from that country live.

I jump to SepiaMutiny.com and Sikhchic.com. I wonder how people know all these things. Must be a lot of researching and a million years in college. The posts on popular culture and entertainment are my favorites. Sikhchic has a film review titled "Dr. King and I" by Valarie Kaur, about Dr. Martin Luther King Jr. The subtitle is "Our freedom is inextricably tied up with the freedom of those next to us."

I'm about to click on it when I glance at the clock. Two a.m., and I haven't even started on my notes for Lesiak's paper.

But this discovering more about myself stuff is addictive. It's like starting a book that you just can't put down, only it's better because the whole book is about *you*.

Chapter 9

In the next couple of weeks, a plane goes down in Queens, New York, and a whole neighborhood is in flames. That sends everyone back into a panic, and rumors go around that the principal is talking about installing metal detectors in the school. After several outraged parents call the school, the vice principal announces over the PA system that this is "entirely untrue." Images of flying planes and fires are once again plastered across TV screens and newspapers.

I go home every night and head straight to my computer. I exchange a few text messages with Mike, usually along the lines of—

Me: hey, im home. hows wrk
Him: ok Same0 lame0 u?
Me: ok
Him: miss u
Me: me 2
Him: wtr u doing 2nite
Me: hmwrk wut els
Nothing for several minutes. Then,

Him: l8r

Me: l8r

And then I get to my favorite part—researching *me*. I've made SikhOut.org my home page. I learn more about being Indian—excuse me, being *South Asian*—than ever before. I download bhangra songs and "Asian fusion" music on iTunes. The more I learn, the more I realize I don't know. It's like I'm getting two educations: one at home for learning about who I am, my history, my culture, and stuff about American history that I never learned in school; and the other at Melville, for learning about everybody else and the official version of American history.

Molly's excited about everything I'm learning too. She even has a favorite bhangra group. But when I blather on about it too long, she starts chewing her hair and looking over my shoulder at people passing by.

Once when I was relaying an online SikhOut discussion to her, I saw her eyes drifting toward a group of guys. I said, "So, Moll, are you a guy or a girl?" just to see if she was listening.

She nodded her head with great interest and said, "Really?"

So I've toned it down a bit with her. But I really wish I could keep blathering on about it.

When I get my most recent calculus quiz back, it's an A–. Molly groans, looking at her C+. "It's *so* unfair!"

I shrug. "If you grew up doing math puzzles and games, you'd be a mathlete, too." I give her a big grin. "It's never too late to start."

"Whatever, Wally."

A warmth blooms briefly in my chest at the sound of her old nickname for me. She hasn't used it in a while. "It's not my fault you're numerically challenged."

She loops an arm through mine. "C'mon, Wally. You know that without your coaching, I am a math *loser*. Besides, I've got better things to do with my time . . . like watch that gorgeous new basketball player. He hangs out with that purple-haired guy . . . the one with the eyebrow ring, what's his name again— Ajay? Anyway, back to our new basketball forward! Have you *seen* him? What a hottie!"

As we get closer to Thanksgiving weekend, I'm like one of those clear balls with bursts of static electric energy at the Science Center. Too much going on in the brain. I have to keep it undercover, so Mom doesn't suspect anything, but inside I'm a disaster. I'm so excited and nervous and . . . *full*, that I'm nauseous.

Molly calls periodically to give me mini pep talks. Every time I get paralyzed at the thought of visiting the people who made Mom's life so unbearable, Molly reminds me of Mom's own words, "Everyone has their own truth." Still, I wonder if they would agree with Balvir and think that I'm a coconut, masquerading as the real thing despite all my research.

By the time Uncle Sandeep calls Thursday morning from our meeting spot down the block, I'm a basket case.

"Relax," he says, fidgeting nonstop with every knob and dial on the dashboard.

Air rushes out of me like an untied balloon. "They made Mom's life hell."

"She made their life hell too."

I remember PunjabiKuri's posts on the SikhOut forum, about not being allowed to shave her underarms, and having to endure all kinds of taunts and hostility. "They didn't let her shave her legs!"

"They're from a different time and place, Samar. They're overjoyed to finally meet *you*, their first and only grandchild."

"What if they're disappointed? What if they think they got cheated—that their only grandchild is a loser who knows nothing about anything? What if they want me to take Punjabi language lessons and go to Sikh camp?"

He glances at me, eyebrows drawn together in the same perma-frown lines that Mom has. "Samar, *calm down*. If they ask you to do something you don't want to do, just say you don't want to do it . . . goodness! They've had to deal with Sharan—you will be a walk in the park for them. Believe me, Samar, they will just be thrilled to see you."

Then he goes into the same serious instructional mode he was in at the gurdwara. And just like then, it does the opposite of calming my nerves.

"When you meet them, Samar, you will greet them in the traditional Punjabi greeting with your hands together in front. You will say '*Sat Sri Akal.*' Ma and Papa are your *Nani* and *Nana*—that's Punjabi for maternal grandmother and grandfather."

I take a shaky breath in and nod.

"But most important," he says, raising a finger, "just relax . . . and give them a chance."

Yes, a chance. This is what I wanted, right? Contact, some sort of connection, my little spot in the jigsaw puzzle, even if it's not fairy-tale perfect. I lay my head back and watch New Jersey blur past my window for the next ninety minutes and try to calm my stomach.

When we arrive at the house, I'm dumbfounded. I don't know what I expected, but this isn't anywhere close. The house is made of stone, a stately mansion type; something I could easily picture Bobbi Lewis living in. There's a "lawn," which is actually more like a mini botanical garden, in the middle of a circular driveway.

We park right outside the front door, and Uncle Sandeep scrambles out. I climb up the stone steps behind him, past the tall white Romanesque columns, to the huge, carved wooden doors. He looks at me, gives me an uneasy thumbs-up, and opens the door with his own key.

The entrance is all white marble with gold accents. There is a huge mirror on the wall to our left, with a gold vine frame. The foyer opens up into a vast hall with a staircase that splits off, one side going to the left of the house, and one side going to the right. There is an enormous skylight above the staircase, making it seem like we're in a bright courtyard.

Descending gracefully from the top of the staircase is a thin, dignified woman. She holds herself erect as her eyes remain fixed on me. Nani. Behind her is Nana, slightly taller, but just as regal as Nani. His shoulders are broad, and his eyes dart a quick glance at me before returning to his wife.

Before I can compose myself, a gasp escapes my lips.

These, at long last, are *my* grandparents. Nani wears a light peach silk salwar kameez, with a cream-colored, translucent scarf embroidered in the same peach as her outfit; and Nana wears a crisp white shirt with light gray wool pants. His turban is cream-colored and wrapped differently from Uncle Sandeep's. Nana's is more round and drapey, whereas Uncle Sandeep's is tightly wrapped and comes to a point at the front, like a boat. Nana and Nani are both wearing brown leather slippers.

Nani comes toward me immediately, arms outstretched. "Samar, *beta*, at long last . . ." Her eyes brim with tears, and she envelops me in her folds of silk and chiffon. I feel like I'm having an out-of-body experience. Everything seems so surreal. The scene I've been wondering about, imagining, secretly yearning for while at the same time dreading, has suddenly sprung to life in front of me.

I put my hands together prayer-style like Uncle Sandeep instructed. "*Sat Sri Akal*," I murmur.

Nana puts his hand on the top of my head. "*Jeethi raho, beti*," he says, and then adds, "God bless you, my dear."

Uncle Sandeep steers us all into a gigantic kitchen, where Nani pours freshly brewed chai tea into four large mugs.

"Samar, *beta*, your Nana and I have waited many years for this moment," Nani begins. "We're overjoyed that Sharanjit has begun to see sense. It's simply madness to keep a family torn. Where is she, Sandeep, still in the car? Why hasn't she come in yet?"

I look at Uncle Sandeep, who reaches a finger under his

turban to scratch his temple. "Uh . . . Sharan doesn't know Samar is here, Ma."

Nani stops stirring sugar into a cup. Slowly she turns to him. "What nonsense is this?" she asks sternly.

"Ma, if Sharan knew, you would never have met your granddaughter. Samar wanted very much to meet you. And you and Papa have been crying for years to see your only grandchild."

"*Hiyo rubba!*" Nani exclaims, slapping her hands together in prayer and looking up at the ceiling. She gives Nana a horrified look and asks, "You hear this, *Ji*?" And then, to Uncle Sandeep, "Sandeep, this is very bad. If Sharanjit discovers this deceit, she will certainly say we had a hand in the treachery!" She steps back from the counter, wrapping her scarf tighter around her shoulders. Splotches of pink dot her cashew-colored face. "*Hiyo rubba*, it will make everything much worse! If there is any faint hope of ever making amends with Sharanjit, you have canceled it today!"

"Your mother is right, Sandeep," Nana booms. "This is *unacceptable*. You must take Samar home and return only with Sharanjit's consent."

I feel like I'm standing on a single, flat stone while everything—all my hopes for this meeting—falls away into oblivion. I blurt out, "But wait! Mom will never agree . . . and I don't want that to stop me from getting to know you!"

Nani cups my face in her hands. "Samar, *beta*, believe me, we will be a part of your life. But not like this. It must be done correctly. If we do not do it properly, we may lose Sharanjit, and *you*, forever. A thought I cannot bear."

Nana shakes his head angrily. "Sandeep, this is your fault! You should know better!"

"Go, *beta*," Nani says, her eyes tearing up. "Go and talk with your mother. Then come back . . . with her, and we will do this the right way."

And that's it. Before I know it, Uncle Sandeep and I are shuffled out the door.

"I'm sorry, Sam," Uncle Sandeep says, once we're in the car and on our way. "They're right. I should've thought it out more. This was wrong, and I'm sorry if I raised your hopes. Papa's right, it is my fault. I'm the adult. I should have known better."

Plan A fizzled before it was even launched. Plan B was a bust. There is no Plan C. I stare out the window and gulp down the tears threatening to burst forth. "It's all a mess," I whisper.

Chapter 10

The Friday after Thanksgiving passes in a daze. I swing back and forth from despair at the way the day unfolded and absolute amazement at finally having met my grandparents. I avoid Mom at every turn and slowly inch my way into the paper for Lesiak.

Every time I approach the assignment, or even try to think about it, there's some sort of invisible force pushing me away.

I go back to the morning of the attacks, but it's like trying to keep a helium-filled balloon on the ground without tying it up. I keep wanting to float away from the memory. I start writing, hoping that it will anchor me somehow.

The first thing I remember is the vice principal coming over the PA system and announcing that, due to an emergency, school would be closing for the day. She advised all students to go directly home. No one knew what was going on, but from the tone of her voice, everyone knew something was up.

The students around me darted nervous glances at one another. The Columbine shootings flashed through my head as I quickly packed up my books from first period. Then, within minutes, it got around: A plane had hit one of the World Trade Center towers. By the time Molly and I grabbed our things from our lockers and headed toward the bus stop, news had gotten around that a second plane had hit the other tower. Molly and I grabbed each other's hands tightly and rushed out of the building toward the crowded bus stop.

But Mom was already outside by the curb, waiting, along with a number of other parents. She grabbed me and held me close for a moment before drawing Molly into the embrace as well. We drove over to the MacFaddens' and watched the horror unfold on TV with the rest of America. There were a lot of tears, cups of tea, and hugs.

Mom and I left when it became too much to bear, and went home to our quiet little house. I wanted to stay with Molly and her family, where someone was always close by offering warmth or a hand-squeeze. I remember crawling into bed with Mom that night, for the first time since I was a little girl.

School was not canceled, but Molly and I, like many other students, stayed home for the rest of the week. Although Mom saw no clients in person, she took some emergency calls from panicked clients who were alone during that time. The days immediately after the attacks were jittery ones filled with a lot of sadness. Molly and I hung out every day, at her place or mine. Mom made us stop watching the news coverage that we had become helplessly entranced by, and she brought home several videos to take our minds off the attacks, if only for a few hours. I have to admit that it did help.

Then, the Saturday after the eleventh, Mom suggested that

Molly and I go shopping for a bit. She dropped us off and went home to have a session with one of her Saturday clients. Molly met up with her dad for lunch, and I took the bus home with my new pedicure kit.

That's when I first saw my uncle Sandeep on our doorstep.

I stop writing for a moment to reflect on my first impressions of my uncle, and the fact that the attacks on September eleventh were what prompted him to seek me and Mom out in the first place. I wonder how Mom could not want to be around her family at a time like that. I wonder why it never occurred to her to seek out her family like Uncle Sandeep did.

I swallow the little pit of bitterness in my throat and turn to the research I've done online. So far, I have about thirteen pages of notes. Balvir was right; there are a lot of similarities between Pearl Harbor and what happened in New York City, but like Uncle Sandeep said, there are a lot of differences, too.

My head is swimming in notes and memories when Molly calls.

"Hey, Wally!"

"Moll! When are you guys getting home?"

"We're driving in late tonight, so come over tomorrow morning, okay? I can't wait to hear all about it!"

"It was awful."

"I know, I got your message. Come for breakfast, okay?"

"Okay. How's it going with Great-Aunt Maggie?"

I can almost hear her eye roll. "Same ol', same ol'."

That girl has no appreciation for what she's got.

The next morning Molly and I are in her room after a breakfast of lemon-ricotta pancakes that Molly whipped up. In theory they should be delicious, but in reality, they're more like lemony Frisbees.

"Go back to your mom, and maybe be a lot smarter about it this time? It's the only logical next step," Molly says, putting the finishing touches on her pinky toenail. She's painting it Granny Smith Apple green.

"If this was *your* mother, that might be the logical next step. With *my* mother, the logical next step is a quick dive off the Empire State Building, Moll."

She drops her head to the side. "It's not *that* bad."

Molly's lack of comprehension is getting on my nerves. "Maybe not for you."

"Look." She stops painting to look up. "You got to meet them. That's what you wanted, right?"

"I want more than that! I want what other people have . . . what *you* have with your family . . . I want my peeps."

She raises an eyebrow. "*Peeps?*" She screws the top back on the polish and blows on her toenails. "It's not all it's cracked up to be, Sam. There's a lot of crap that comes with the package." She waddles on her heels to her dresser. "What color do you want?"

"Fine—give me the crap. I want the whole package . . . black."

She pulls out the squeeze bottle of henna she bought from the tattoo shop in town. "You have no idea what you're asking for . . . people nosing into your business, giving you their opinions on everything you do, from your hair to your toenail polish to your boyfriends . . . where do you want it?"

"Just underneath my collarbone." I pull my sweater down from the neckline. "You don't seem to understand. I want people in my business . . . people other than my self-centered, egotistical mother. If it's just me and her for the rest of my life, I swear I'm going to make that trip to the Empire State Building."

"Then you have to come up with a new plan." She squeezes the thick liquid onto my skin in curlicues and soft ripples. It's a design I picked from ones she has in her portfolio. That's her secret. Although her parents want her to be a lawyer, Molly's real talent is beauty.

"Or go back to Plan B," I say miserably.

"Don't move," she says, dabbing a cotton ball soaked in lime juice and sugar water on the raised henna tattoo. "You have to hold your sweater like that for at least thirty minutes."

"No way." I squirm out of my sweater. "Do you have a sweatshirt with a zipper up the front?"

She throws one next to me. "Plan B means convincing Uncle Sandeep again."

"That might not be as hard," I say, slipping my arms through the sweatshirt. "He wants this as much as I do, I think."

"Which is why he doesn't want to piss off your mom." She stands back, admiring her work. "Nice," she says with a pleased nod. She pulls out another bottle of henna mix, the one that leaves a deep tangerine stain on the skin, and grins, wiggling her eyebrows up and down. "I like the authentic stuff." She starts a design on her forearm, from the inside of her elbow to the inside of her wrist.

I watch her work for a moment. She's completely absorbed in the lines and dots she squeezes out of the bottle. She lays the final squiggle down with a flourish.

"Gorgeous, Moll," I whisper.

"Thanks," she says, holding her arm out and appraising it. "I hope that new basketball player notices. Diego, I think his name is."

"I'm sure he's noticed you already, Moll."

She looks up. "Hey, what's going on with you and Mike?"

"He had Thanksgiving dinner at his cousin's. I'm going to see him tomorrow night."

"Are you guys all right?"

I shrug. "I don't know. Things seem . . . different somehow."

She nods. "He seems different now that he's working all the time."

"It's something else, too. He's got a problem with Uncle Sandeep, and—"

"What kind of problem?"

"I don't know. He just seems pissed off and bitter all the time."

"Hmm," she says, looking down at her arm again. "Gotta watch out for that."

Mike's mom is home when I arrive for dinner on Sunday night. All the windows are open, and she's fanning thick smoke out of the kitchen. "Hello, Sammy! Come on in, I'm burning dinner."

"Hi, Mrs. Brezinsky." I take off my coat and start fanning the fumes with her.

She laughs. "Looks like we'll be ordering pizza!"

Mike stomps down the stairs. "Hey, Sam," he says, bending down to brush my lips with his. "I'm calling Nonno Frankie's. Any requests?"

"Mushrooms!" his mother shouts over the exhaust fan.

I shrug. "I'm easy."

He gives me a "yeah, right" look and goes to the living room to order. I follow behind him and tuck my legs underneath me on one end of the big cream-colored leather sofa. Mrs. Brezinsky collapses next to me.

"It would've been a perfect soufflé," she says, brushing mahogany strands out of her eyes.

I look at her hair, the color of rich earth with thick white roots tangled throughout, and how it bleeds into warm mahogany about half an inch up from her scalp. I give her a reassuring smile. "I'm sure it would have, Mrs. B."

She sighs and nods, the slender fingers of one hand raking her hair back. Her face, which on a good night is as pale as the moon, is even paler tonight, making her Cindy Crawford mole rise like a little black hill at the corner of her mouth.

"Mmm," she says, crossing her legs. "What's on television tonight, anything good?"

Mike hangs up the phone and clicks the remote. He flips through until he lands on *The Simpsons*, one of his favorite shows.

His mother swings her top leg slightly. "How was your Thanksgiving, Sammy? What did you and your mother have?"

"My mom's not big on Thanksgiving." I say, smoothing my skirt down over my thighs. "She sometimes makes a small dinner for us, or we order in early before everything closes."

"Oh," she says. "Well, we went to visit one of Mike's cousins in Pennsylvania for the day."

"It sucked, as usual," Mike mutters.

She gives him a look. "It wasn't so bad, Michael."

He keeps his eyes on the TV. "It *was* so bad. Every year's the same—Judy gets pissed drunk and yells at Bob for cheating on her ten years ago, Laura cuts her kids down in front of everyone, and we all hate each other by the time it's over."

She purses her mouth. "There are good parts to it too."

"Yeah, the booze."

The doorbell rings. Mrs. B. gets up to answer it. "That's not funny," she says over her shoulder.

"That was fast!" she says flirtatiously to the delivery guy.

Mike rolls his eyes and says loudly, "They're around the corner, Mom."

"It was still fast," she snaps.

I reach across to touch Mike's arm. "How's work?"

"It's all right," he says, pushing the recliner back. "They're piling on the work before the holidays, so everyone's doing twice their share, or more. But we don't get paid overtime, we get to bank the time and take it off later, in order of seniority."

His mother comes in with the pizza and some plates and napkins. She sets everything down on the coffee table in front of us. "Seems like that's the scene everywhere," she says.

"Phil Taylor and Todd Hamilton got fired last week. The company's hiring illegals under the table for pennies a day."

His mother shakes her head. "I hope they tighten those borders like they said they would. Especially now—it's such a scary world out there."

My stomach clenches. Phil Taylor . . . Rick Taylor's brother. I nibble at my slice.

Homer Simpson's at the Kwik-E-Mart, and Mike cracks up when Apu Nahasapeemapetilon, the Indian owner with a heavy accent, starts talking. I put my slice down and stare quietly at the screen.

I've watched Apu at least a dozen times before with Mike and never had this feeling. I never thought it was uproariously funny like some of the kids at school or Mike did, but it never really bothered me either. Or did it, and I just ignored it?

I think of Nani and Nana with their heavily accented, proper English. What would Mike think when . . . *if* . . . he ever met them? Would he see pride and dignity? Or would he see Apu at the Kwik-E-Mart? And Uncle Sandeep? Even though he has no accent, there's the beard and the turban. What would Mike see?

I feel a swirling, sinking feeling. A feeling of being exposed, and at the same time, completely invisible.

"What's up, Sammy?" Mike asks. "You haven't touched your pizza."

I look at the slice. "I'm actually not feeling well."

Mrs. B. looks at me in concern. "Let me get you something. Pepto-Bismol, Midol, Tums . . . ?"

I shake my head. "I think I need to go home."

"Are you sure?" she asks, brow wrinkled. "Maybe if you lie down for a moment . . . ?"

I shake my head again and put my hand on my roiling belly. I try to breathe, to calm myself down.

"Come on," Mike says, getting up. "I'll take you."

Mrs. B. helps me on with my coat, and Mike takes my hand.

The frigid air feels good when we step outside. He looks at my face as we walk to the car. "You gonna hurl?"

I shake my head.

"Got diarrhea?"

I smile in spite of myself. *"No."* Mike's ability to make me smile under almost any circumstance is one of the qualities that hooked me on him in the first place.

We get into the car and he turns the heat up full blast. "If you fart, I'm opening *all* the windows. Let's get that straight right up front." He looks at me with his goofy grin, the one that kicks my temperature up a notch.

I roll my eyes, still smiling a little. "It's not gas."

"Then what is it?" he asks, pulling out of the driveway and onto the main road.

I stop smiling and stare out the passenger-side window. "I don't know. I guess it's just . . . I don't think *The Simpsons* is that funny."

He gives me an "are you crazy?" look. "It's hilarious. *That's* why you're feeling sick?"

My stomach flips again. "I don't think it's funny to make fun of that Indian guy. . . ."

"You're joking, right? Tell me you're not serious."

I say nothing.

"Sammy, it's a *cartoon*. They're laughing, joking, ha-ha . . . get it? The show makes fun of everyone!"

"I know, but . . ." I look at my knees, then turn to look at him. "It's not funny . . . *to me*." In my mind, the image of Mike coming face-to-face with Nani and Nana and their Apu-like accents sprouts tall and dark, like a giant fir tree blocking the sun.

He leans back in his seat. "You're changing, Sammy."

I stare at him, my mouth ajar. "I'm changing? *I'm* changing? Mike, no one has changed as much as you have in the last year! You are nothing like the guy you were when we first met—ask anyone! Even Molly has noticed. . . ."

"So you and Molly talk about me—about what a jerk I am?"

"No, it's not like that. . . ."

I see the muscle at his jaw jump as he steers with one hand. "Well, maybe we've both done some changing. You used to be way more fun. Now you're way too serious . . . you can't even take a joke. I mean, come on—*The Simpsons*? *Everybody* thinks it's funny. Let loose a little. Life is too tough to get that serious." He pauses. "Is it your uncle?"

There's a note in his voice that sends a chill through all the layers I'm wearing. A chill that wakes something up inside me.

"This has nothing to do with my uncle," I say coldly. "This is about me . . . seeing things differently—more clearly—than I've ever seen them before."

"Oh, really."

"Yes, *really*."

"So you're seeing things 'more clearly' now that you're talking to Molly and your uncle is around, huh? What else do Molly and your *uncle* think?"

"You know what, Mike? I've had enough." I will myself to breathe evenly, but I clutch the door handle for strength. I've never been good at endings. "Stop the car."

"What?"

"Stop the car." I'm a good hike from home, but I have to get out of the car. I can't breathe.

He looks at me like I've lost my mind but pulls over to the curb. "You're nuts."

He could never understand that this is the least nuts I've ever felt. "I think we're done, Mike," I say softly. Every inch of me, including my lips, is shivering.

"You're joking, right?"

I unbuckle my seat belt and open the door.

Mike grabs my wrist. "What does Molly know? She doesn't know me the way you do, Sam . . . and your uncle, he's a friggin' stranger. You know nothing about him . . . and you've been with *me* over a year!"

"Let go, Mike. This is not a competition!" My heart thumps wildly in my chest as I drop one leg on the ground.

He squeezes my wrist in a vise grip, fury raging behind his eyes. "Fine," he says. "Get out, then."

He drops my wrist and I scramble out the door and onto the sidewalk, swallowing huge gulps of icy air. His car screeches away, leaving the smell of burning rubber stinging my nostrils.

Chapter 11

Whether from the cold, or from breaking up with Mike, I'm still shivering like a wet kitten when I get home. The house is dark and silent. There's a note on the refrigerator: *Sammy, going out with Abby and Leslie after Women in Transition group tonight. Chicken fried rice in the fridge. School tomorrow—bed early!*

I crumple to the floor, still in my coat, scarf, and hat. Giant sobs rock my body. I press my forehead and palms flat against the tile floor, whimpering as entire threads of who I thought I was liquefy and leave my body as tears. I feel as if deep roots are being cleaved from my depths, without my permission.

When the heaving finally stops, I wipe my eyes and nose with my scarf, curl up like a shrimp, and fall into a deep, merciful sleep.

I wake to Mom shaking me. "Sammy, wake up! Are you okay, sweetheart?"

I look around in a daze and nod my head. "I must've fallen asleep."

"My God! I came in, you were on the floor, face all puffy, curled up like someone had punched you. . . ."

I hold up a hand. "I'm okay, Mom." I pull myself up, wishing I had thought to fall apart in my room.

"Sammy . . ." She gently grasps my shoulders. "I know you're upset with me, and I don't know what happened tonight." Her chin quivers. "But *please*, honey . . . let me help."

I lean against the countertop as the scene with Mike replays in my mind. Fat tears roll down my face and splatter onto my socks. "I had a big fight with Mike" is all I can get out without wailing.

"Honey," Mom says, sounding almost relieved. She wraps her arms around me. "I'm so sorry!"

Feeling her softness, breathing in her scents—cardamom, vanilla, coconut, almond—transports me back to when I was little. When I was teased at school or got a scraped knee on the playground, right here in Mom's arms was the only place I wanted to be.

I dissolve into her embrace.

"Come," she says, helping me off with my coat and taking my scarf and hat. "I'll make us some hot chocolate." She pulls down the tin of cocoa and puts mugs of milk in the microwave.

I drop gratefully into a chair. Mom's back is turned as she scoops heaping spoonfuls of cocoa into the milk and stirs. A wave of exhaustion washes over me. It's too much. Everything has been too much for me to handle on my own. In the past, Mom was always there to nudge me along with a word or a look. We were like a Dynamic Duo, fighting the forces of evil all on our own. And it was fun when I was a kid. But I'm not a kid anymore, and I need a much bigger world.

Mom brings the steaming mugs to the table and sits down across from me. "This'll help, sweetie." She warms her hands over her mug. "Do you want to tell me about it?"

I trace the handle of my mug. "I broke up with Mike tonight."

"Aw, honey, I'm sorry. You'll go through the normal grief cycle, and it'll hurt for a while, but I promise you it'll pass—"

I interrupt, before she gets going full steam on the grief cycle. "There's more, Mom."

She wrinkles her brow. "What is it, honey?"

I'm either really stupid, or super, super tired, but something about fighting with Mike tonight, and remembering that time he snickered and said, *What is it? Uncle So-deep? Or is it Some-deep?* gives me a kind of courage I've never felt before. I'm more determined than ever to find out about the tree I branch off of. I've heard Mom say that it's often easier to defend someone you love than to defend yourself, which is probably true. It didn't bother me as much when people made fun of my last name as it did when Mike made fun of Uncle Sandeep's name.

I draw an unsteady breath and rally my inner troops. "Your parents," I begin, "my grandparents . . ."

She sets her mug down. Her gaze is unwavering as she waits for me to continue.

"I know you never want to have anything to do with them. . . ." I trail off. I don't know how to say what I really want to say. I don't know what I want to say. Then I remember what Ms. Lesiak said right after the Trade Center attacks: *One baby step at a time. You only need to see as far as your next step.*

I take another deep breath and keep going. "I know you had a really tough time growing up with your parents, Mom. But I deserve a chance to get to know *my grandparents* . . . and see what they're like for myself." I pause again to collect my thoughts.

"I know you're doing your best and you want to protect me . . . and you've always been good at that . . . but I just want the chance to . . ." I sigh in exasperation.

Mom stays silent. Her gaze is unsettling.

I plod on. "Mom, most people never get to know their grandparents because they're dead, or they live too far away. Mine are alive and well, and only a ninety-minute car ride from here . . . and I don't even know them! And now, especially after September eleventh, it just seems so . . . I don't know, *important* for me to know my own family."

Her eyes flash. "You *do* know your family, Sammy. We are a perfectly valid family unit."

Wrong word choice. "I know, I know," I say quickly. "You always drove that home. Even on Father's Day, you made sure we were around lots of other 'families without fathers' so I didn't feel different or less than anyone else. I meant to say family as in a *family tree*—a history. Something that goes back past you, way back . . . something that I'm a part of."

She sits quietly for a few moments. "I suppose," she says finally, "that if I don't agree, you would go ahead and do it anyway."

Heat races throughout my limbs. "Um, about that . . . ," I mumble.

"Hmm?"

I clear my throat. "About that . . ." I gulp. "I convinced Uncle Sandeep to take me to meet Nani and Nana."

She stands straight up with her palms on the table. "You *what*?"

"I know I should've asked you, but . . ."

She purses her mouth, eyes flashing. But she stays quiet.

Still, I flinch as I say, "It was all me. He never would have agreed if Molly and I didn't ambush him."

"Molly was with you?"

"We double-teamed him."

She closes her eyes and throws her head back, crossing her arms in front. "You deliberately went against my wishes," she says slowly, shaking her head.

"If I hadn't, I never would've met my grandparents!"

She levels her gaze at me again. "You might have, if you'd approached me with some of the maturity you've displayed this evening."

I slump miserably in my seat. "I didn't have it before."

She sits down and taps a fingernail on the table. Then she leans back and covers her face with her hands. "Aaaarrrrghh, Sammy!" she says finally, throwing her hands in the air and sitting up in her chair.

She rests her elbows on the table, looking evenly at me. "I thought I gave you such a strong sense of family. I did everything in my power to make up for the absence of what's-his-name and my parents. . . ."

I open my mouth to speak, but she holds up a hand to shush me.

"But it's not enough. I can see that. I wanted to protect you, Sammy, not deprive you. If having a relationship with your grandparents is what you *really* want . . ."

I nod my head vigorously. "It is, Mom, it is. I want to have my own relationship with them, even if it's not perfect, even if it's awful."

She stares at the backs of her hands, then looks up to meet my eyes. Her eyes are like little dark wading pools.

"I'll call them," she says with resignation.

I can't believe my ears. Did she just say she'll call *her parents*? "Wait—what did you say?"

She chews on her bottom lip. "I can't promise anything, or make any guarantees. . . ."

"Really?" I couldn't care less about guarantees or promises— Mom said she'll call her parents!

"As long as you go into it with your eyes open, Sammy. It's very important for you to be aware of what you're dealing with. I'm not sure you fully understand. . . ."

I leap out of my chair and walk around to her side. I kneel down next to her. "I'm ready, Mom. I can take it. And I'm not expecting any miracles."

Okay, not entirely true. I may not be *expecting* miracles, but I'm definitely *hoping* for them. I would love to have the kinds of big, huge, happy family gatherings that are advertised in Hallmark commercials, with lots of Kodak moments in between.

She takes a deep breath and exhales loudly. "Okay, then," she says, reaching out to cup my chin. "I promised myself after what's-his-name left that I would not let anyone hurt you. I'm going to stick by that promise, Sammy." Her voice is tender, but firm.

"I know, Mom." I lean my cheek into her hand. "But I'm a big girl now. You can't keep running interference for me."

She leans back and drains her cocoa. "I'll work on letting you be. But you have to understand that you are my baby, and when you get hurt, every single ounce of me wants to make it all better, in whatever way I can."

I give her a teary grin. "I'll take that."

When I crawl into bed that night, I wrap the covers tight around myself. I want to go over the conversation I just had with Mom, but I pass out before I can recall a single word.

Chapter 12

can't believe Mike would act like that!" Molly says. "And your mom's gonna call your grandparents? How freakin' cool is that? I told you she's a cool mom."

"Yeah, you did say that." I take a pair of eyelash curlers out of Molly's makeup bag.

"Ouch!" Her shout almost kills my eardrum.

We're in the bathroom before first-period bell on Monday morning.

"Hey!"

"Sorry. Grabbed some skin instead of hair."

"I can't believe you're plucking. You have no eyebrows, MacFadden."

"I'm *shaping* them. It says in *Cosmo* that well-shaped eyebrows can give your face a whole new look."

"Huh. I saw that on *Tyra* once too." I toss the eyelash curler back and pull a tube of lip gloss out of the front pocket of my bag. "I've got butterflies—no, *dragonflies*, Moll. I'm so freaked out about Mom's call. What if it goes terribly? What if it makes things so much worse than they already are? What if this puts the final nails in the coffin and they hate each other for good?"

"Wow . . . I hope that's not how it goes down. It'll probably be just fine, Wally. At least it's something, right? They're not just sitting there not talking . . . there's actually going to be some real, live contact."

I dab lip gloss on my bottom lip and toss it back into my bag. "That's true. It's something. But I'm so messed up inside about it."

"I would be too. Especially with the night you just had. What is up with Mike, anyway?"

My heart falters at the mention of his name. "I don't know . . . it could be me, too, I guess."

"I don't know, Wall. Ever since he left school he's been turning into a whole different person."

I shrug. "I sorta freaked over an episode of *The Simpsons*."

"The Simpsons? As in Jessica?"

"No. As in Homer and Bart."

"Um, not that that gives any guy a reason to be a jerk, but . . . why would you freak out over Homer and Bart Simpson?"

"Not Homer and Bart—Apu . . . the Indian guy from the Kwik-E-Mart. The one with the thick accent."

She's silent for a long moment. Finally she says, "So what ticked you off?"

I fling my bag over one shoulder. "It's just not funny to me anymore, I guess."

Another silence as I hold my breath. *Please don't fight me on this, Molly.*

Then she says casually, "I never thought it was funny."

A smile tugs at the corner of my mouth as I exhale quietly.

"Check out my eyebrows," she says without skipping a beat. "Don't they look awesome?"

Mike has left five messages on my cell phone since last night. I finally give in and dial my voice mail after first period. My heart does this stuttering thing and my knees almost give way. So funny how as soon as you have a fight with a guy, all you want to do is climb all over him.

Mike and I have had fights before, but never like this. He's usually cool. He never gets physical like he did last night. A shudder zips through me as I remember his hand clutching my wrist. And then, *Fine. Get out, then.*

Tears prick my eyes as I hear his voice. But his messages are not apologies. It's almost as if a whole night hasn't passed since his last words to me.

The first one is short: *"What goes around comes around, Sam."* What the hell is he talking about?

The next one is more furious. *"This is nuts! You break up with me cuz of a TV show? Everything was cool with us till your uncle showed up and you started listening to your friends instead of using your own brain."* Tension seeps into my neck and shoulders. I open the double doors into the school and start walking to my locker. My legs feel like cement blocks.

In the next three messages, his speech is increasingly

slurred. There are voices and party noises in the background. *"I bet you think you're too good for me now, don't you? There's nothing special about you, Samarrrr . . . Samarrr the math genius, Samarrrr the good girl, good in school, good at home, good in bed . . . not!"* That message is followed by loud, raucous laughter in the background.

And finally, the last message. *"Yeah, so now you got your fam-uh-lee, huh?"* He raises his voice to mimic a woman's, slurring heavily now, *"Oh, I'm seeing everything sooo clearly now, Mike. My family . . . I'm changing! I'm soooo big and important!"* Then he laughs callously. *"Who needs you, anyway . . . you cold . . . bitch."* He mumbles incoherently for a few more seconds before hanging up.

I hit the end button with rigid, trembling fingers.

As soon as Molly breezes into a seat next to me in calc class, I slide my phone onto her desk, set to Mike's first message. "Check this out," I say, jaw set.

Bobbi Lewis walks in as the bell goes off and plunks into a seat on Molly's other side. Molly smiles and gives her a quick wave as she listens to Mike's first message. As the messages play, her expression goes from puzzlement to dismay, to outright shock and disgust.

"Un-freaking-believable!" she shouts at the end of Mike's last message.

Lim stops scribbling on the board and turns. After a quick burst of snickers and hoots, everyone quickly bends their heads over their notebooks again.

"Any more outbursts, and I will come up with a quick spot quiz that will count toward your final grade," Lim threatens, turning back to the board.

Molly looks at me, passing my phone back. Her mouth is a perfect O. She tears off a piece of paper from her notebook and quickly scrawls a note, then hands it to me. *What an asshole! Unbelievable!*

I nod and turn to my notes. The numbers blur in front of my eyes. How could I have missed this part of Mike? Was it always there and I just chose to ignore it? Or is it something new, like Molly says—some weird mean streak that's oozed into him since he left school?

At the end of class, Bobbi leans across to Molly. "Coming to biology?" she says, laying a hand on Molly's shoulder.

Molly nods and turns to me. "Want me to walk with you to your next class?"

I nod. "Okay."

She turns to Bobbi. "I'll catch up with you."

We drift with the throngs headed in the direction of my class. I know this will make Molly late for hers, but if it keeps her away from Bobbi Lewis, even if just for a few minutes, it's worth it.

"I can't believe that jerk!" she says as soon as we're out of calc. "Just ignore him, Sammy. He was obviously drunk and out of his mind."

I swallow the stone in my throat. "I've never been called that by a boyfriend before, Moll. Unless it was as a friendly joke. And even then, it feels mean."

She nods in agreement. "I know. Guys shouldn't be allowed to use that word, *ever*. Especially with their girlfriends."

We stop outside Lesiak's classroom. Balvir passes us on her way in. "Hey," she says, snapping her gum.

"Hey," I say.

Molly nods and turns back to me. "I'll come to *your* locker after school, since your track record isn't the greatest in that area." She gives me a quick squeeze and takes off in the opposite direction, toward biology with Bobbi.

Lesiak zeroes in on me as soon as I walk in the door. "Samar, do you have something for me?"

Heat rises to my face. "Um, actually, I . . . uh . . . don't, Ms. Lesiak." I set my backpack down on a desk and shuffle through it. I pull out my notes and walk to her desk.

"I've been working on it, though, and I would like to make an appeal for an extension."

She flips through the pages of notes with all my scribbling down the margins and looks up. "All right. You have until the end of the week, Samar. But I will still have to deduct one letter grade."

I groan.

"Or we could go back to deducting one letter grade per day. . . ."

"End of the week it is." I slink back to my desk.

For the rest of the hour, we talk about how Gatsby tries to reconcile decadence in the elite circles of New York, how Daisy Buchanan's voice is "full of money," and what that means.

At the end of class, Balvir walks over and sits in the empty seat next to me. "Hey, did you get to check out SikhOut?" I notice she pronounces it as "seek out."

I gather my books and give her a lopsided smile. "Yeah . . . it was pretty cool."

She grins. "There are some real wackos on there, but most of the people seem pretty cool, right? I'm UltraBrownDiva."

I smile. "Cool handle."

"You?"

I'm not sure I want her to know my online name yet. I might choose to post something someday, and I don't know if I'd want Balvir to have access to some of my innermost thoughts.

"I haven't got one yet. I might, but right now I'm enjoying surfing the posts." We walk out of class together. "You know, I never really grew up Sikh. My mom sort of jumped ship after she got married."

"I don't blame her. It's not an easy road for any of us, obviously." She points to her hair and the makeup she applied this morning at school. Then she walks me to my locker. I throw my books in and grab my lunch, then we walk to her locker.

"My mom cut off *all* ties to her family," I add.

She nods. "That *is* pretty drastic." She grabs her lunch and we walk to the same spot we sat in last week, opposite the football field.

"How do you deal with it?" I don't specify what "it" is, but I don't have to.

"My folks?" She shrugs, taking a bite out of her bagel. "I

guess I do what I want anyway. What they don't know won't hurt 'em."

My plan to visit Mom's parents behind her back flashes through my mind. I stare out at the thick, dark clouds above the empty field. "What if it's not something you can hide? My mom wanted to marry someone her parents didn't approve of. Then she got really pissed off and wanted to have nothing to do with any of her family." I take a bite of my banana.

"Sounds like either your mom's parents were really strict, or she's a true rebel—'Give me freedom or give me death!'" She grins. "I can't remember who said that . . . some revolutionary." Then her voice goes serious again. "My parents are really strict too, but I'm the youngest of three girls. Your mom sounds like my oldest sister. She took off and married a white guy, so my parents had to mellow out with me and my other sister." A light rain begins to drizzle. "They said that as long as my other sister and I marry Indian guys, they're happy . . . but God forbid if they're Muslim or Hindu." She pauses and raises her eyebrows in surrender. "I have a whole checklist for potential boyfriends . . . and I still have to come to school early to change."

"My mom married an Indian guy . . . but he wasn't the *right* Indian guy," I say into the falling drops.

The rain comes down harder. Balvir gets up, laughing, and holds a hand out to help me up. "See? We just can't get it right, can we?"

After school, Molly meets me at my locker. With Bobbi. I give her a look that is at once questioning and dagger-ish. When

Bobbi turns to chat with a friend, Molly grabs my elbow and leads me away a few steps.

"Just do it for me, Sammy," she says through a clenched smile. "It's in our social best interest to be seen with her." The three of us walk out of the school together, with Molly in the middle.

"I'm on the committee for the Midwinter Dance," Bobbi babbles. "It's the third week of January this year."

She natters on. When she finishes, I start up about my paper for Lesiak. For the next fifteen minutes, Bobbi and I take turns talking only to Molly. Finally she gets annoyed.

"Look, you two, you have a lot in common. Can we cut the crap and just hang like regular people? What's your problem with each other, anyway?"

I look at Molly in disbelief. "You're out of your mind, MacFadden," I say, and walk faster, breaking away from them both.

"Sammy!" she says, catching up with me. She goes on in a low voice, "Sure, we've both had problems with Bobbi in the past, but . . . just *talk* to her. She's not bad—she's actually kind of cool."

I stop walking. Bobbi walks several feet behind me and Molly. "Look, Moll. I don't know about you, but I happen to recall, quite clearly, some of the names Miss Bobbi Lewis called people all throughout grade school . . . mean, nasty, hurtful names! And if I remember correctly, you were right there with me when we used to talk about how mean she is! Now, all of a sudden, you want her for a friend. Okay, MacFadden, you got her. I'm good." I keep walking, and Molly stops to wait for Bobbi.

I walk for the next several minutes without looking back, but I know Molly and Bobbi are not close behind because I can't hear either of their voices. I slow down when I round a bend, fuming at Molly's notion of a great idea. What would make her think I want to be friends with Bobbi Lewis? We both hated her in grade school. Her stuck-up, snotty attitude, flashing all the latest trends, looking like she just stepped off a European runway, and now, driving her own powder pink Lexus to school. We were two of a handful of brown—or at least brown*ish*—girls in our school, and she never gave me the time of day. She would walk past me like I wasn't even there.

I glance over my shoulder. Still no sign of them. I keep walking but slow down just a bit more. Molly has gone completely bonkers. What could she possibly think we have in common? Bobbi Lewis and I couldn't be more different!

A car rolls up alongside me and slows to my pace. A black Honda Civic. My insides contract and icy fingers take hold of my throat.

Mike leans toward the passenger side, yelling out of the open window. "Hey, Sammy! Can we talk?"

The whole world is going nuts. "After those messages you left on my voice mail? No way."

"Sam, c'mon . . . I was wasted, I didn't know what I was saying!"

"You called me a . . ." I walk faster. "*Forget it*, Mike. I am not getting in the car with you." Feet pound behind me. I whip my head around, and Molly and Bobbi almost knock me over.

"Sammy, are you okay?" Molly says, out of breath.

"She's fine," says Mike, rolling his eyes.

"I didn't ask you," she fires back.

"This is between me and Sammy," he says heatedly. Then to me, "Sammy, just get in. I'll take you home."

"I'm almost there. Leave me alone, Mike. You didn't leave us much room to talk after those messages."

"Oh, come *on*! I told you I didn't know what I was saying."

Suddenly Bobbi turns to him. "Didn't you hear what she said? She said NO. Now buzz off!"

"Yeah, Mike," Molly adds. "You said what you had to say . . . we *all* heard it."

Mike's face flushes cherry red. He clenches his jaw and looks me dead in the eye. But he says nothing. Instead he peels away, leaving black dashes in the road where his wheels were.

Molly shakes her head. "Un-freaking-believable."

The three of us walk in silence until we reach my driveway. I hug my books to my chest and look at the ground. "Thanks."

Molly gives me a tight squeeze. "Thanks for what? If that was me, you would've done the same, except you probably would've been more violent." She grins.

I nod. "True." I turn to Bobbi and mumble, "Thanks."

She smiles sympathetically. "I went on two dates with Simon Monroe early this year, and he didn't understand the meaning of the word 'no' either."

"Simon Monroe?"

She shrugs. "He's hot and smooth, but get in a dark room alone with him and it's octopus city."

I give her a slight nod and say good-bye before turning to walk up my driveway. Bobbi misunderstood my surprise about Simon. I'm not surprised he's a jerk. I'm surprised she didn't know it before she went out with him. I thought it was obvious to everyone. But then, there's a whole lot about Mike I never saw before too.

I look back at Bobbi and Molly walking down the street. A girl like Bobbi could have anything she wants. She grew up in the wealthy part of Linton, her father's one of the only African-American golf players in the area, and her mom is the director at the Institute for Jewish Research and Studies.

She has always been surrounded by pretty, expensive things, and pretty, expensive people. Molly, on the other hand, buys most of her clothes from thrift shops and has one trusty, loyal friend—yours truly.

I can see why Bobbi would want to hang with Molly. And after the way Bobbi stood up for me with Mike, I'm starting to wonder if I should do like Molly says and give Bobbi the benefit of the doubt. Maybe that's why Uncle Sandeep tries so hard to be understanding all the time.

If we give them a chance, people could surprise us. Maybe if we didn't make up our minds right away, based on a few familiar clues, we'd leave room for people to show us a bunch of little, important layers that we never would have expected to see.

Chapter 13

The rest of the week I go straight to my computer after school and work on the assignment for Lesiak. Somehow, after I get past the first part—remembering that day—the rest of it sort of tumbles out. Like it has been sitting there all along, just waiting for me to get it.

I do the title last: "American Heartbreak: A Personal Account of a National Tragedy." When I print out the final, clean copy, I feel a huge sense of accomplishment and relief. I have a finished paper that I'm actually proud of, despite losing a letter grade and taking forever to get to it.

I read the first sentences over again:

> Is it possible to feel completely American as well as completely un-American? After September eleventh, I never felt more un-American in my whole life, yet at the same time, I felt the most American I've ever felt too. I never knew

it, but really, this has been a recurring theme throughout my life and it seemed to get shoved into my face after the attacks on the World Trade Center.

I catch a snippet of Mom's telephone conversation downstairs and stop reading to listen.

"Sandeep, where Sammy is concerned, you have to respect *my* rules. . . ."

I tiptoe to the top of the stairs and strain to hear more.

"Mm-hmm . . . mm-hmm. You're right, I shouldn't have said that. . . . I know you don't. . . . No, no, you're absolutely right, that wasn't fair of me. . . ."

She mumbles a few words, so I go down a couple of steps. "You ought to know me better than that, Sandeep. I want my daughter to be proud of who she is. It was never my intention to keep her from getting to know her history. . . ." She turns on the exhaust fan and it swallows the rest of her sentence.

I sigh and go back to my room, little acid bursts going off in my stomach. A moment later Mom calls me downstairs. I take the steps two at a time.

"Sammy," she says, leaning against the counter, "I had a conversation with Sandeep."

As if I didn't know. *Aaaaand?*

She bends to pick up a cookie crumb. "We decided the best time to take you to visit . . . your grandparents . . . is when everyone is off from work and school. That puts us into the

Christmas break. It'll give me, and you, a little time to prepare, as well as work out anything that comes up. Plus, I need to work myself up to call them and arrange everything." She walks stiffly to the trash can to throw the cookie crumb out.

I swallow hard. As nervous as I am, I know Mom's got to be freaking out. Suddenly it feels like there's not enough room for both of us in this house.

"Can I go to Molly's to finish my homework?"

She gives me a nod, and I turn to sprint up the stairs. "Sammy?" I look back at her.

She hesitates, then says quietly, "Let me know if you need anything."

"Okay," I say, dashing upstairs to call Molly.

As I race to Molly's house, scenes of disaster play through my mind. Mom screaming at her parents, Uncle Sandeep and Mom embroiled in a shouting match, Nani and Nana discovering how un-Indian I am and throwing both me and Mom out . . . My stomach knots up and I move faster, trying to outwalk the adrenaline. Every so often a car rolls past, and I whip my head around, thinking it might be Mike. It doesn't help that there are so many black cars on the road. The very thought of Mike makes me cramp up.

"We have the whole place to ourselves," Molly says when I get there.

I shrug out of my coat and drop my backpack. "I'm totally freaking, Moll."

"Wanna drink?" she says, grinning mischievously.

"A *drink*? Are you kidding? I have to get this homework done, I'm already way behind as it is."

"So, this'll help you relax. Come on, Sam, how're you going to focus on doing any work if you don't relax a bit?" She goes to her parents' liquor cabinet and pulls out a bottle of Cuervo Gold and two shot glasses. She raises her eyebrows, eyes sparkling underneath.

She's right. A tiny bit might help me loosen up a little. "Okay, but just a *teeny* bit."

She smiles and flits off to the kitchen. When she comes back, she has a salt shaker and a couple of pieces of lime. We sit cross-legged on the living room rug, and she hands me the salt shaker. "Lick the back of your hand." She licks her own, takes the salt shaker from me and sprinkles salt on the wet spot.

I stare at her in amazement. "Where did you learn this?"

"I have cool cousins." She takes a piece of lime in one hand, licks the salt from the back of the other, grabs the shot glass, downs it, then immediately sucks on the lime.

"Wow . . . Impressive." I take a deep breath and mimic her movements. I immediately see why the lime and salt are necessary. My throat feels like it's been seared.

She nods. "I know, right? Should we do another one?"

"Um, I think I'm okay." My voice comes out raspy.

She gets up to put the tequila bottle away and comes back with a bag of Oreos and a pint of Häagen-Dazs ice cream.

"Maybe this'll help our throats," she says.

I giggle. "Good plan." I lean back against the sofa and close my eyes. Molly's house feels warm.

She plops down on a cushion next to me and hands me a spoon. "Still freaking out about your mom . . . and visiting your grandparents?"

My stomach immediately makes a fist. "Crap. Yeah." I dig into the dulce de leche.

"Don't worry, Wally. It's gonna be okay. Whatever happens, at least it's *something.*"

"I guess." Molly was right: The ice cream feels good sliding down my throat. Before I know it, my spoon is scraping the bottom of the container.

Molly smacks her lips. "Should we have some more?"

"Thought you'd never ask."

We polish off another pint of ice cream, the Oreo cookies, and a bag of Cheez Doodles before watching a couple of episodes of *Fashion Faceoff* on DVD.

As the credits roll, I glance over at the untouched textbooks on Molly's dining table. "Crap, Moll, we haven't done any homework."

She pushes herself up against the sofa and groans. "I know. I guess we'll have to get up early and do it."

Somehow, now that my paper for Lesiak is done and I won't lose any more letter grades over it, I don't feel as worried about the textbooks we never got to.

By the time I pull on my boots, there's not a trace of our drinking "adventure"/pig-out session in sight. The empty ice-cream containers and bags of snacks are in a trash bin behind the house, the shot glasses are washed, dried, and placed back in the liquor cabinet, the bottle is back behind a bunch of other bottles, and the lime pieces are in a plastic sandwich bag in my backpack.

"Sorry I wasn't much help, Sam. I know you're freaking out. Maybe we should go shopping this weekend?"

I give her a hug. "Hanging out and watching *Fashion Faceoff* was a big help. Got my mind off all the big stuff. Plus, ice cream is always a bonus." I flash her a grin. "But nothing helps like shopping."

I step out into the chilly air. A black car at the corner catches my eye, and I go rigid.

"What's up?" Molly asks, face wrinkling in concern.

"I thought I saw . . ." I shake my head. I must be seeing things. What would Mike be doing sitting on the corner by Molly's house?

"Never mind, it's nothing," I say, and hug her good-bye.

The air feels good on my face as I begin walking. I breathe deep to shake the eerie feeling from my bones.

After a couple of blocks, I hear a car slow down behind me. This time I avoid the impulse to turn, and keep walking. But it doesn't drive past. I turn around and Mike's Civic pulls up.

"Hey, babe," he says, rolling down his window. His words are slurred.

I halt, gripping the straps of my backpack.

"Want a ride?" he asks, smiling. But it's not a smile I've seen from him before. It's more . . . mocking.

I pull my zipper up to my chin and shove my hands into my pockets. I turn to keep walking, and quicken my pace. "Mike, I said leave me alone."

"I can't leave you alone. You're my girlfriend."

"*Was* your girlfriend."

"What the hell were the two of you doing in there?"

I keep walking briskly. Mike is creeping me out, and my legs are ready to sprint. "The two of *who*? What are you talking about?"

"You and your *girlfriend*. What the hell were you two doing for all that time, all *alone*?"

My heart lurches into my throat. I stop and turn slowly to look at him. "That was you at the corner. Were you watching us, Mike? How long were you sitting out there?"

He ignores my questions and stops the car. "What else am I s'posed to do? I gotta do *something*. You won't call me back, you won't get in my car—you're my girlfriend, what d'you think that makes me look like?"

My eyes bulge out, and I'm about to let him know exactly what else he's supposed to do, when he opens the door. There's a half-empty bottle of Jack Daniels on the seat next to him.

He staggers out onto the sidewalk and wraps his arms around me. "I miss you, babe."

I clench my teeth and squirm away. "Mike, *get off me*." But he has my arms pinned against my sides as he gently pulls my head back. He drops his mouth on mine and tries to push my lips open with his.

I turn my head to the side, so he catches my ear between his teeth. "Mike! Get *off*." Finally, after he makes no move to let me go, I kick him as hard as I can in the shin.

He lets go and shouts, "Aw, f—!"

When he reaches for me again, I take off, power-walking through lawns and staying away from the road. I'm not afraid that Mike's going to hurt me, but I am totally weirded out by the fact that he sat outside Molly's house until I came out.

When I get home, Mom takes one look at my face and says, "What's the matter?"

I let the door slam behind me and lock it. "Mike . . ."

She wrinkles her brow, and stops flipping through her *O* magazine. "Mike what? Did he do something to you?"

Against my better judgment, I start babbling. "He's doing really weird things . . . like he sat outside Molly's house the entire time I was there, then followed me, and—"

"He what? He's stalking you?" Mom grabs the phone, pulls aside the curtain, and examines the street outside our window.

"Yes, I'd like to file a restraining order," she says into the mouthpiece.

A restraining order? I try to stop her. "Mom . . ."

She holds up a finger and drops the curtain. She puts an arm around me, walking me to the couch in the living room. "No . . . no . . . this is the first time, as far as I know. . . ." She covers the mouthpiece with her hand. "Sammy, has this ever happened before?" I shake my head. She continues into the phone, "No . . . What do you mean? *Repeated* attempts? You've got to be joking. . . . Since when? Proof? What *kind* of proof?" She listens for a few more minutes, then quietly clicks the phone off.

"Mom, I don't think he was going to hurt me. . . ."

"That's not the point," she says firmly. "He sat outside Molly's while you were there, then he followed you. That qualifies as stalking. Who knows what else he's capable of doing?"

I stare at her reflection in the blank TV screen as she paces the kitchen, breathing heavily and crossing her arms in front of her chest. True, I'm a bit creeped out by Mike's impaired judgment . . . but a restraining order?

She picks up the phone again. "I'm calling that boy's mother."

I head up the stairs as Mom dials Mike's number. She covers the mouthpiece and calls after me. "Honey, if you're hungry, there's eggplant—still warm!" I go to my room and stare at my books in a daze, then pull out my cell phone to call Molly.

"Hey," she says after the second ring.

"Mike sat outside your place the whole time I was there."

She gasps. "He *what*? No way. How do you know—did you see him?"

"He followed me when I left."

"Did he do anything? Oh, Sammy—I *knew* we should've called your mom, or waited till my parents came home so they could give you a ride!"

I lower my voice. "Yeah, right. That way, they could've gotten a real good whiff of all that 'studying' we were doing."

She groans. "I know . . . are you okay? What happened?"

"He got out of the car and was all over me. He was wasted, Moll. I saw a bottle of Jack Daniels on the seat next to him."

"He was driving drunk? What a genius, driving while impaired, and underage. . . . He didn't hurt you, did he?"

"No. But how weird is that? It's just so creepy to know that someone's following you."

"And sitting outside—*waiting for you to come out!*"

"My mom went ballistic."

"Well, *yeah.*"

"She's downstairs right now, calling his mom. She called the cops before that."

"Wow, the cops . . . I guess that's good. Bobbi's right, what the hell is it with these guys and the word 'no'? Everything's fine till you use that one little word, and then they go insane. I bet Mike wouldn't be so freaked out if he was the one who dumped you."

Mom calls up from downstairs. "Sammy!"

"Gotta go, Moll."

"'kay, call me later."

Mom holds the phone out to me as I come down the stairs. I approach it cautiously. "Who is it?"

"Michael's mother."

My heart falters as I raise the receiver to my ear. "Hello?"

"Sammy, I'm so sorry for Michael's behavior. He's stressed out at work, trying to help me get these damn bills under control, and I guess he's taking your breakup pretty hard. I'll have a talk with him. Don't worry, he won't be following you home again."

"Okay." I'm not sure what else to say.

Mom takes the phone from my hand. "Thanks again, Sylvia. Mm-hmm . . . will do. Bye."

She turns to me. "I still want you to watch it, Sammy. Poor

Sylvia is doing her best, but young boys Mike's age are pumped up on hormones and very unpredictable."

I nod and grab the banister. As I walk back upstairs to tackle my homework, I wonder if Mom is overreacting, or if I'm underreacting. My own judgment seems to be a bit impaired lately.

Chapter 14

The weeks race toward the holiday season. At times I wish they would slow down so I could untangle some of the feelings inside me. Other times, I wish it would all just hurry up and be over with already.

Today we're having more Healthy Discussion and Debate in Lesiak's class. She picks up a pile of papers and walks slowly to the front of the room.

"I'm handing back some of your papers on the attacks in September. I'd like you to read a few paragraphs out loud to your classmates so that we can generate dialogue. Shazia, here's yours. . . ."

Just as I'm praying that I won't have to read mine, she sets it down on my desk. "Samar . . ."

Wonderful. The last thing I need right now is to bare my soul to my classmates.

Lesiak goes back to perch on a corner of her desk. "Samar, why don't you start us off?"

No, thanks. I look down at my paper for a long moment.

"Go ahead," she gently prods. "We'll be hearing from others as well. You're not alone."

I stand up and swallow what feels like a plum pit in my throat, scanning the paper for the part I want to read. "I never thought before about who I am—"

A girl at the back interrupts. "I can't hear!"

"A little louder, please, Samar."

I sigh and begin again. "I never thought before about who I am and what my history is. Then 9/11 happened. I would have felt awful about it anyway, just like every single one of us, but it was even bigger than that for me, because my uncle showed up on my doorstep a few days later. The last time I saw him was when I was two.

"My Uncle Sandeep is Sikh and wears a turban. Ever since 9/11, he's been harassed, yelled at on street corners, had garbage thrown at him, and been mistaken for the current Public Enemy Number One: Osama bin Laden.

"Being with my uncle puts what happened in New York City on September eleventh in a whole different light. He's one of the gentlest, coolest people you could ever meet. He wouldn't hurt a fly, but he constantly gets linked to one of the most violent and destructive images of our time.

"Seeing what he goes through reminds me of . . ." My voice cracks and I drop my paper. It flutters onto my desk.

"Just finish that paragraph," Ms. Lesiak says softly.

I take a breath and continue. "Seeing what he goes through reminds me of some of the things I went through when I was younger. Things I had shoved way back to the dusty, shadowy parts of my mind. Being with him makes me want to know who I am, where I come from, and what the rest of my family is like. He's kind of like a road map for me. If I look at him real close, listen, and tread carefully, I'll find my way home." I blink back tears as I float back into my seat.

"Thank you, Samar. I know that wasn't easy," Ms. Lesiak says. She looks at the rest of the class as I sit down. "None of these papers were easy to write, were they?"

Lots of nods. "They're not going to be easy to read out loud in class, either," someone mutters loudly.

More nods and mumbles of agreement.

"It wasn't easy to write, or read out loud, I'm sure," Tina Volpe agrees from the other side of the room, "but hearing Sam read hers really made me feel better somehow . . . like I'm not the only one who's having a hard time with it."

Lesiak nods. "Anyone else?"

Shazia speaks up with her deep, silky voice. "It's good," she says resolutely. "This class is like a microcosm of the world with all the different opinions. It's vital to hear what other people think. At least that way, you can address it and get closer to the truth. If no one talks to each other, all we know is what we hear from the media."

"I agree," Nick Kiriakos says from the back. "It doesn't make anything better, but it helps to keep you going."

Several other students read paragraphs from their papers throughout the rest of the class, and it's true. Listening to the different ways everyone is struggling and coping helps in a way I can't quite figure out. It's like shattering little, brittle, glass walls between us or something and being able to breathe a bit better. Or like a huge group hug. There's a real feeling of closeness and warmth in the room toward the end of class.

Lesiak glances at the wall clock and stands. Her face looks like Mom's when she's trying not to hug me. "You have all done a fantastic job with these papers. We will keep this discussion alive and come back to it from time to time throughout the rest of the year. However, in the meantime, please read on in Fitzgerald's *Great Gatsby*. . . ."

Balvir gives me a thumbs-up and an approving nod from her seat, a couple of rows over, before she heads out the door.

I go through the rest of the day swinging in and out of the movie screen in my mind. So many things are swimming around in the soup that my brain has become.

I gaze out the windows of my classrooms and see black Civics on the road. Sometimes I squint to catch their license plates, but usually they're moving too fast. Ever since the incident with Mike, I've made it a point *never* to walk home alone, especially when it's dark out, which happens to be really early these days.

A couple of weekends before the start of the holidays, Molly and I make it to the mall for some retail therapy.

"Oh my Gawd, Sammy, I am *so* in love." Molly's going on about Diego, the basketball player she has some serious hots for.

"Oh yeah—how'd your date go the other night?"

"Can't you tell? You'd never know it from those big, rough hands, but he's got this feather-soft touch." She caresses her cheek with the back of one hand and closes her eyes.

I grab her elbow and steer her toward Victoria's Secret. I have a free panties coupon that I want to cash in, and this trip to the mall is supposed to help get my mind off going to Nani and Nana's house next weekend. Not an easy task, since all the disastrous possibilities keep snapping back into my brain like a rubber band.

"Shake it off, Wally," Molly says sternly. Ever since I filled her in on more details about Mom walking away from her family, Molly has taken to using my childhood nickname more often. It does help a little.

"Shake what off?"

"You know exactly what," she says, one hand on her hip. "We're here for some retail therapy, and there's no better place for that than *here*." She waves around the store. "Vamanos."

We split up, and I halfheartedly browse the racks of teddies, slips, bustiers and bras. I give up when memories of Mike's hands and mouth exploring my skin burble up in my head—when it was all *good*. I sigh and walk to the section where the free panties for the promotion are stacked up. I pick out a bland pair of tan ones and head to the cash register to meet Molly.

She opens her bag to show off a red, flowery, satin slip with matching mules. I raise my brows. "What possessed you to get those?"

She shrugs. "I've always wanted them, and these were just cheesy enough."

"They're too big to fit in your little box of lingerie—how're you going to hide them from your mom?"

"I'll separate them and slide them up top in my closet, along with my Reproductive Anatomy and Human Biology textbooks," she says with a wicked grin. She looks at my bag. "What did you get?"

I open the bag so she can see my underwear.

"That's it?"

"Um, in case you forgot, I don't have much need for lingerie right now."

"So? You will again, soon."

I shrug. "I guess I just wasn't in the mood."

"Oh, Wally," she says, draping an arm around my shoulders.

We walk to the food court and Molly goes to Amato's for pizza, while I go to the Big Fry.

"Remember the last time we were here?" She slides into the seat across from me and dives into her garlic bread. "We did a pretty good job double-teaming Uncle Sandeep," she says, coming up with a parsley mustache.

There's a commotion at the other end of the food court, and we turn to see what's going on. An Indian girl, about our age, with a long braid down the middle of her back, is being dragged down the hall by her ear, away from a mortified Indian guy—also about our age.

The girl screams, "Ow! We weren't doing anything, Dad! We were just talking!" while the man says, "How dare you disobey me! Talking to boys. You'll get a reputation and ruin the family name. Everyone will have trouble marrying their children off because they're related to you!"

"Wow," breathes Molly. "Talk about intense."

I look closely. Something about the girl looks vaguely familiar. The walk, the voice . . . I sit up straight as a jolt zips through me. I didn't recognize her right away because she's out of slutty, retro, alter-ego gear. Instead, she's sans makeup, wearing muted browns and grays (totally covering all body parts), with her hair pulled tightly back in a braid and her eyes cast down.

I whip my head toward Molly at the same time that she turns to me, mouth wide open with half-chewed pizza. "It's Balvir!" we exclaim in unison.

"I can't believe it!" I say. "I didn't even recognize her."

"How could you? She doesn't look anything like the girl we know at school."

I shake my head in disbelief. "Could you imagine? Being dragged away, publicly humiliated, just for *talking* to a guy?"

Molly's eyes are wide as she stares down the hall where Balvir and her father were moments ago. "Not at all."

We sit quietly for a moment. I stare at my uneaten french fries.

"I wonder if that's what life was like for my mom with her parents." I look up at Molly. "I wonder if she ever had any scenes like that . . . if that was the reason she wanted nothing to do with them."

She chews slowly. "Wow," she says again. "I wouldn't want anything to do with them either, if they were like that."

"What if they're still like that? What if they're awful tyrant dictators, just like my mom said they were when she was growing up?"

Molly shrugs. "Well, then that's what you'll find out. And you don't have to live with them like she did. You can come back home and never deal with them again."

My shoulders sag. "Then I'd be right back where I was before . . . before anything was even a possibility."

"Anything, like what?"

"*Anything.* Now it's all a possibility. I could *possibly* have a huge family waiting to get to know me, a place to go every year for holidays and celebrations . . . just like you do. Memories and cool cousins and funny pranks . . ." My voice falters. "Or I could have nothing. I could end up back home with Mom and our two-person birthday dinners, and Cornish hens for Thanksgiving. And this time, no Mike, either."

She tilts her head to one side, turning the corners of her mouth down. "Don't worry," she says, "it's gonna be fine."

Somehow, I'm not totally convinced.

The week leading up to the visit to my grandparents' house is strange and surreal. My feet never feel like they're making full contact with the ground. It's almost as if I can't really feel the outside world because I'm trying so hard to keep up with my inside world. And inside is a commotion that rivals tsunamis and earthquakes.

Mom, on the other hand, is a complete wreck. The Saturday before the visit, Mom double-books not one, but *two* clients. Then, a day or two later, she leaves her wallet in the fridge.

When she pours orange juice onto her Flax Power cereal, I say, "Uh, Mom . . . are you sure you want to do that?"

She stops midpour and collapses into a chair. "Oh, dear," she says, shaking her head.

"Are you okay?"

She gives me a weak smile. "I should be asking you that."

"I'm more worried about you." This is true, but not in the way it sounds. I'm not worried about my mother; I'm worried how her reunion with her parents is going to go. I'm worried that it could blow up in all our faces. I'm worried that it could be a blast so bad that I could be worse off than before. That it could go terribly wrong and end up with Mom forbidding me to go anywhere near my grandparents—or Uncle Sandeep, even. I put my hand under my belly button to soothe the sudden feeling of tightness inside.

"Thanks, sweetie," Mom says, getting up to dump her cereal out. "I'll be fine . . . I just need to relax a little."

I have my doubts, but I leave it alone.

It's not until she walks out of the house in her socks one morning that Mom finally calls her former therapist, Tina. As part of her training during the master's program in social work, Mom had to go through her own therapy. Every morning I'd come downstairs for breakfast, and she'd be furiously scribbling away in her dream journal. This was supposed to help her "get in touch with her subconscious self." Sometimes I'd walk in after school and see her speaking to a cushion on an empty chair. It gave me the creeps a bit, but she explained that it was all part of learning to "let go and move on." Still, I'm glad she doesn't do that anymore.

When I get home on Wednesday afternoon, Mom says,

"Sammy, I have a telephone session with Tina, so could you take care of dinner on your own tonight?"

"Tina? Your old therapist?"

She sighs. "Yes, Sammy. I thought it might be a good idea for me to have somewhere to go with . . . with all the feelings that are coming up for me around the visit to see . . . your grandparents. I've scheduled two ninety-minute sessions with Tina. I know how important this is for you, but it's not going to be easy for me. I will do my best, but I can't promise anything." She looks like she wants to say more but bites her lip instead.

I nod, wishing I could turn around and go back to school, to Molly's, to Victoria's Secret . . . *anywhere.*

Mom takes a step forward and gives me tight hug. "Oh, Sammy . . . is there any way I can make this easier for you?"

A bunch of answers crowd my mouth: You can be nice to your parents; you could've not cut me off from my family; you could've been nicer to my dad; you can stop trying to run my life so much . . .

Instead I shake my head.

She kisses me on the forehead before going upstairs.

I have to admit, though, that the sessions with Tina seem to do Mom a lot of good. By the time Friday evening rolls around, she's much calmer. She's almost back to the solid, confident Mom I know.

Almost.

The Saturday before Christmas, we're off to visit my grandparents.

Chapter 15

The ride there is uncomfortable and seems to have no end in sight. It didn't seem this long when I was with Uncle Sandeep. Mom and I drive in silence for the most part, except for the radio and Mom's "soothing" CDs. It's a perfect December day, brimming with sunlight and a brilliant blue sky—what Mom once called "blue like a peacock's neck."

When we get to the house, I'm again overcome by how huge and stately it looks. Sort of like a visit to the White House or the Taj Mahal, maybe, or one of the Wonders of the World. At least to me. Uncle Sandeep is already there; his car is parked just over to the side, like he left Mom and me the prime parking spot, right outside the front door.

Mom waits a beat before opening her door. She takes a deep breath and gives my hand a squeeze, then we both climb out. I was nervous the first time I came here, but that pales in comparison to being here with Mom. Part of me wants to climb right back into the car and go home, but this is too important. No. I straighten my spine and march up the steps behind Mom.

After a quick glance at me, she rings the doorbell. The shadow of a turban bobs toward the door. Uncle Sandeep flings it open, grabs Mom in a bear hug, and lifts her off the ground. She yelps and gives him a boot to the shin. "Sandeep, put me *down*."

"Sorry, Sharan. I've been looking forward to this moment for so long." He drops her and lets her regain her composure, then greets me with a similar hug, though more careful not to drop me. Then I notice Mom stiffen.

Nani and Nana enter the foyer. Nani is again in flowing chiffons, this time an avocado green, and Nana has on a freshly pressed, banana-colored shirt and pants. His turban is a warm, chocolate brown.

Nani seems to float majestically toward Mom, like a sailboat. She raises her arms and engulfs Mom in the same embrace she had folded me in the last time I was here. That huge plum pit lodges in my throat again.

Mom, still in her coat and boots, stands rigid for a few seconds. Then, bit by bit, all that stiffness comes crumbling off. Years of rage and bitterness yield to the salt of tears. Mom brings her arms around Nani's waist and lays her cheek on the older woman's gently rounded shoulder.

In all the years I've been with Mom, I never once thought of her as somebody's daughter. That was my role. Obviously, I knew she *had* a mother, but it never really sank in that she was a daughter too—somebody's little girl. It never once occurred to me that she might want to lay her own cheek on a mother's warm shoulder, the way I've done for years with her. A tear wriggles down my face.

Both women sob softly while Nana and Uncle Sandeep stand awkwardly off to one side, hands shoved deep into their pants pockets. Nana clears his throat several times, looks up at the skylight, then pretends that something is in his eye. Uncle Sandeep is beaming, his eyes damp and shiny.

When Mom and Nani disentangle themselves, Nani turns to me. "Samar, *beta*, come here," she says, bangles jingling as she motions me forward. She has a magnetic pull, something at once firm and gentle, which commands obedience.

"*Sat Sri Akal*," I say with my hands together, prayer-style, the way Uncle Sandeep showed me last time we were here. Nani pulls me to her chest, murmuring something in Punjabi. She smells like cloves and cinnamon, and something else, something a lot like Mom's smell.

I begin to sob, and not nearly with the delicate beauty and grace that Mom and Nani showed a moment ago. Nana gruffly orders Uncle Sandeep to "fetch a box of tissue," which Uncle Sandeep is only too relieved to do. Nana puts his hand on the top of Mom's head in blessing. "*Jeethi raho, beta.*" Then he does the same with me.

Uncle Sandeep comes jogging back and shoves a box of Kleenex toward Mom, Nani, and me. "Anybody hungry?" he asks brightly.

"*Han, han,*" Nani says. "Sharanjit . . . Samar, *beta*, take off your coat and boots. Dinner is already on the table."

Mom hangs up our coats and scarves, and lines our boots neatly on a mat by the door. Nani leads us through the hallway to the right, and Nana and Uncle Sandeep bring up the rear. There are colossal paintings that I never noticed before, of Sikh Gurus on the walls, depicting scenes of war and meditation, serenity and struggle. There are captions underneath each painting in both English and Punjabi, about the specific historic event each painting shows.

I read the names of the Gurus in the hallway as we pass them: Guru Gobind Singh Ji on his horse, with a bow and arrow slung on one shoulder and a white falcon on the other, and Guru Tegh Bahadur Ji and Guru Arjun Dev Ji, both meditating peacefully. In the dining room, which is bigger than our living room and kitchen put together, there are more paintings of gurus. I walk closer to read the names at the bottom of the images: Guru Nanak Dev Ji, Guru Angad Dev Ji, and Guru Amar Das Ji.

There are no women. I try to look at the house through a Mom-lens. What must it have been like to grow up in this home as a little girl? As a teenager? What were Nana and Nani like, say, twenty-five years ago?

We arrive at the table, which could easily seat ten. It's already laid with beautiful dishes of steaming Indian food—all vegetarian. Again, I'm astounded by the bigness of everything.

Nani and Nana sit on one side, next to each other. Mom and I sit across from them, and Uncle Sandeep sits at the "head" of the table, though it's clear where the real "heads" are seated. I look at the spread: mattar paneer (mine and Mom's favorite), kidney beans (which I have learned is Uncle Sandeep's favorite), a big garden salad, dal, rotis, rice, cucumber raita, lime pickle, mango juice, salty lassi, and a pitcher of ice water.

Nani closes her eyes, breathes, and in a low voice says,

"*Satnam, Sri Waheguru Ji.*" After which she promptly starts doling food onto a plate. She loads the plate with small amounts of everything and hands the first one to Nana, who begins to eat right away. I look at Mom; it's a rule in our house to wait for everyone to get their food before we start eating, but she's staring at the wall hangings. Nani starts on a second plate, which she hands to Uncle Sandeep. He waits. The next one is for Mom, then mine, and finally for herself.

There's an awkward silence when we first begin to eat. I catch Uncle Sandeep darting looks around the table. He catches me watching him and smiles. Then, in a move completely uncharacteristic of the Uncle Sandeep I've grown to know, he sticks his tongue out. I widen my eyes in surprise and look quickly at Nani. She continues to eat quietly. I grin at Uncle Sandeep and stick my tongue back out at him.

"I see Sandeep is up to the same nonsense with Samar that he was up to with you, Sharanjit," says Nani, still looking at her plate.

My face gets hot, and I shove a paneer into my mouth. When I steal a look at Nani, I see the hint of a smile on her lips. It feels as if everyone at the table breathes a sigh of relief. The ice has been broken.

"Not quite," Mom says. "He was much worse when we were kids—he's toned down some in his middle age."

"Middle age!" Uncle Sandeep exclaims in horror. "Woman, bite your tongue!"

Nani makes a roti-spoon and fills it with dal. "I am glad to hear he has toned down since his days of flying off roofs."

"Ma!" Uncle Sandeep groans. "Must we discuss this in front of Samar? She has a young and highly impressionable mind."

"No, let's," I say, hungry for stories. "I'd love to hear about when you flew off of roofs!"

Nani smiles, finishes chewing, and leans toward me. "Your uncle and Sharanjit were outside in the back with their cousins Amrita and Inderjit. Somehow the girls, Sharanjit and Amrita, convinced the boys, Jit and your uncle, to go on the roof of the tool shed with umbrellas . . . and jump. Like that Mary Poopins."

"Poppins, Ma, Poppins," Uncle Sandeep says.

Nana snorts and shakes his head. "Fools," he says, spooning more raita onto his plate.

"We were *five* years old," Uncle Sandeep says defensively. "They told us we would float down."

The corner of Mom's mouth curls up just a tiny bit. "Of course, the umbrellas turned inside out and both boys came crashing to the ground."

"I broke my ankle, and Jit almost lost an eye," Uncle Sandeep says bitterly.

"Oh, you both had a few scrapes and bruises," says Nana. "You were fine."

"Your mother was sadistic," Uncle Sandeep says. "She derived a great deal of pleasure from tormenting me."

Nana turns to Nani. "Remember that time he had a bean stuck in his nose? How old was he then?"

"That's it," Uncle Sandeep says. "If I had known this was going to be a Roast Sandeep dinner . . ."

"Oh!" Nani whoops. "How could I forget?"

"Oh my God, I had completely forgotten that," Mom says.

"Tell me," I say eagerly.

"You, Sharanjit," Nani says, wiping her eyes.

"It was a kidney bean," Mom says, eyes glinting evil as Uncle Sandeep huffs next to her. "I told him I could put it farther up my nose than he could. I never had any intention of putting anything in my nose, and I certainly never thought Sandeep would do such a thing. But of course, never one to back down from a challenge, Sandeep shoved the bean as far up his nostril as he could."

"I could have died!" Uncle Sandeep grumbles.

"You would not have *died*," Mom says, and then giggles. "You just had a bean stuck up your nose."

"He came running to me, screaming and in tears," Nana says, shaking his head. "*Ooloo* . . . I had to hold one side of his nose closed with this thumb"—he holds up his right thumb—"and tell him to blow hard out the other nostril. Couple of times we did as such, and finally it was dislodged."

Uncle Sandeep pushes the food around on his plate. His shoulders are hunched over, and yet, in spite of the scowl on his face, a smile dances in his eyes.

Mom makes a disgusted face. "Papa made me get the tweezers to pull it out. Luckily I didn't have to use them. *Yecch*." She shudders.

The table lapses into another silence. My mind races with ways to squeeze more memories out of all of them. There's so much more I want to know. The family life, friendly banter, and sharing growing pains—hearing these stories gives me some of those missing puzzle pieces.

"So many memories in this old house," Nani says, sighing. "It will be sad to leave it."

"Leave it?" Mom asks.

"We're selling," says Nani.

"You're selling the house?" Mom asks, fork pausing midway to her mouth.

"It's far too big for just the two of us," Nana says.

"Yes." Nani nods. "We originally bought it with hopes of grandchildren running through the rooms, but . . ." Her voice trails off.

After another awkward silence, Nana clears his throat. "Samar, *beta*, what are you studying in school?"

My stomach drops from having the spotlight thrown so suddenly in my direction, and I wonder what the right answer is. "Um . . . well, we study everything. . . ."

"She's in high school, Papa," Mom says smoothly. "They study everything. In college she'll pick a focus."

"You must have a favorite subject, *nah*?" Nana insists.

"I like history . . . and English," I say slowly.

"Hmm." He nods, looking into his glass of water. "History, English."

I get the feeling that was definitely *not* the right answer.

"You will go to university, *nah*?" asks Nani apprehensively.

"Yeah . . . ," I say.

"Good," she says. "Education is very important. How are you doing in school? Straight A's?"

"Well . . ." I'm not sure how detailed I should be with this answer.

"She's doing fine, Ma. Sammy's been an honor student her whole life," Mom says in an end-of-discussion tone.

But Nani persists. "Which universities are you considering?"

Mom blinks in irritation. "Ma, can we drop the interrogation, please?"

"I can't ask my grandchild about her life? I've been kept away from her and now I can't ask simple questions?" Nani says, unyielding. Nana shifts in his chair while Uncle Sandeep bumps his kara bangle rhythmically on the table.

Mom's eyes flash, but she says nothing more. And Nani doesn't pursue the matter further. I finish the food on my plate and sneak a glance at Nani. She looks like an older, fairer-skinned version of Mom. She has deep frown grooves on her forehead. The gold from her pendant and rings glints as she sops up the last of the food from her plate.

"Nani . . ."

She turns and stares at me, her eyes pinning me to my chair. "*Ji,*" she says. "Nani-*ji*, Nana-*ji*, Uncle-*ji*, Mommy-*ji* . . . You must always address your elders respectfully with *ji*, Samar."

"We didn't even say Papa-*ji* and Mommy-*ji* growing up," Mom says quickly.

"We should have been stricter about that," Nani . . . Nani*ji* says. "But Samar can learn the proper way. When she interacts with other Indians, she needs to know how to address her elders." She turns to me and her eyes soften. "I will teach you, *beta*. There is time."

Mom turns to me, her face hard, as if set in plaster. "What were you going to say, sweetie?"

Stunned by the force of Naniji's "instruction," I scramble around in my brain for what I was going to say. "Oh . . . um, I—I wanted to know if there were any family photo albums."

"What a delightful idea!" Naniji says, clapping her hands loudly.

Uncle Sandeep jumps on it too. "Fantastic idea!"

"Why don't we move into the living room?" Naniji says, sliding her chair out and standing up. Nanaji wipes his beard and mustache and gets up to follow.

The living room is in the opposite direction, on the left side of the house. We walk back through the hallway, past the front door and the split staircase and into the living room. There is a sectional peach-colored sofa, a gold-rimmed glass coffee table, and a gigantic television. There is a brass vase with peacock feathers fanning out over each side of the sofa. On the walls are stunning Indian cloth paintings.

"Those are batiks from South India and Sri Lanka: women at the well, women weaving cloth, churning butter, grinding flour," Naniji says, pointing to each painting. Then she walks to a painting of another guru. "This is Sri Guru Nanak Dev Ji, the father of Sikhi."

Uncle Sandeep and Mom are already on the sofa, going through one of the photo albums they pulled out. Nanaji is pulling another one from a chest underneath the bay window that looks out front.

"Oh my God, look at that hair!" Mom says in horror. I rush to sit next to her, and she quickly covers the photo.

"Oh no, you don't." Uncle Sandeep shoves her hand away. "Not after all your mouth flapping over dinner!"

I look at the picture of Mom with bright red, perm-damaged hair teased up to about six inches above her head. I have never seen Mom look like that. We have no pictures at home of this period in her life, and she always looks so composed and self-assured that this photo immediately has me in giggles. Naniji peers over my shoulder.

"That was the beginning of her rebellious stage," she says with a frown.

"What stage? She's still there!" Nanaji says, bringing over another album.

I soak up the images, the tidbits and sound bites, as we go through the albums. "This was during the trip to Niagara Falls." "Look how skinny your cousin Pradeep is here!" "That was my favorite birthday shirt." I see Mom at six, wearing loud prints and checked brown and orange pants, smiling broadly at the camera with her piano teeth; at ten, smiling pleasantly in a Raggedy Ann dress.

Then, at thirteen, the smile becomes just a small fraction of the crescent it used to be; her braids hang limp at the sides of her face, and her hands are folded in front of her on her lap.

But the photos of a teenage Mom are what hold me riveted. Mom and Uncle Sandeep both grow quiet. There are no smiles in these photos, and the spark in Mom's eyes is gone. She stands hunched or staring off in the distance, almost as if she doesn't notice the camera. The teenager in these photos is nothing like the Mom I've known my whole life. Nothing like the Mom in the photos we have at home—Mom with her fist raised at a Take Back the Night march, or smiling with two fingers held up at a peace rally. Mom with her eyes crackling in dissent. *My* mom.

I stare in disbelief at the photos, then look at my mother, and back again. No matter how hard I try, I can't see that bleak teenager in the woman sitting next to me.

She points to the last photo in the album. "This was the day before I shaved my head," she says quietly. She turns the page, and a small photo falls to the floor. I pick it up and turn it over. There, smiling blissfully back at me, is Mom, standing next to a man I know must be my dad.

I gasp and hear Mom's sharp intake of breath next to me. The photo is slightly discolored and a little dog-eared, but it's whole and complete. Mom and Dad on the day of their marriage.

The halls of the courthouse are blurred behind them, in stark contrast to the shimmering excitement in their eyes. Mom has on a lustrous, fitted, silver-gray mermaid dress that reaches just above her ankles. She wears a dazzling bindi on her forehead, and there are tiny rhinestones following the arch above her perfectly plucked brows. Her hair is carefully swept up on top of her head and fastened with fresh flowers. Her lips are a deep ruby color, and tiny pearl earrings dangle from her ears. She stands in his arms, one hand on his chest, the other around his waist, and smiles radiantly at the camera.

He stands next to her, both arms around her waist. He looks dapper and handsome; tall and velvety dark in his suit and tie. His hair is slicked back into a tight, shiny, black ponytail, and he has a ruby flower on his lapel, the same color as the flowers in Mom's hair. He, too, beams joyfully at the camera.

I feel my throat beginning to close up as Mom takes the photo from my hand. She looks up at Naniji. "Why would you keep this?"

Naniji keeps her gaze level, sharp pain clearly evident in her eyes. "It was the last photo we ever received from you."

"But . . . but I thought you *hated* him," Mom says, just above a whisper.

"Han," Naniji says softly, "but he is not the only one in the photo."

Mom stares at the picture in her hand. "This was when it was good," she says, her words packed with static.

"We tried very hard to warn you, Sharanjit. . . . He didn't have a stitch of ambition, and he was absolutely un—" Nanaji gives her a look, and Naniji stops herself before turning away.

Mom holds the photo for a moment longer between her thumb and forefinger, gently, like a cracked raw egg. Then she places it back in the album where it was. A brief silence follows. Uncle Sandeep delicately takes the album away from Mom and opens the next one.

"Ah! Look at cousin Rimi!" he says, opening to a page from earlier years.

Mom's still quiet, but she manages a small smile. "That was one smart girl. She knew how to get us in and out of trouble so fast, it would make my head spin."

Naniji turns back to look at the photo. "Yes," she says, "very smart girl—she went to Harvard, you know, married a very wealthy fellow."

"Good for her," Mom says tersely.

I'm still fighting the surge of tears that threaten to pour forth. That was the first photo I've ever seen of the man who fathered me. Seeing it here, after seeing all the other photos of Mom, makes it hard to get enough air into my lungs. I take a deep breath to quell the feelings fighting forward. Mom covers my hand gently with hers before taking a deep breath herself.

"Never would have thought it of little Rimi," Naniji continues with a chuckle. "But if you're going to be dark, I suppose you have to be smart."

Mom's face goes taut and her eyes flare. "What do you mean, 'if you're going to be dark'?"

Naniji sighs and straightens up to her full height. "I mean that being dark is already an imperfection in our culture. You know that, Sharanjit. Right or wrong, that is the way it is."

Mom snaps the album shut.

"Sharan," Uncle Sandeep begins, but Mom is already standing up.

I drop my head into my hands, my whole body trembling uncontrollably.

"This is *exactly* why I didn't want anything to do with you,"

Mom says quietly. "It's bad enough I had to go through my whole life listening to this garbage. But now I've walked my daughter straight into it too."

Naniji looks at Mom in dismay. "What . . . ?" she says, holding her hands out.

Nanaji gets up too. "There's nothing wrong with being dark, Sharanjit, that's not what your mother is saying."

Mom explodes. "Then *what*, Papa? What is she saying? Please tell me, because maybe I've been wrong for thirty-seven years!"

Naniji folds her arms across her chest. "I did not make up the rules, Sharanjit. Indians all believe light skin is prettier than dark skin—and as much as you would like to, you cannot place that entire burden on me. It has been so since before I was born, and it is still so."

"That does *not* make it right," Mom fires.

"Okay, let's not bring up the past again. Let's move on. . . ." Uncle Sandeep puts his body between Mom and Naniji.

"No," Mom says, walking brusquely to the closet. "We *cannot* move on. This kind of nonsense is precisely why we *haven't* been able to move on. This was the reason you thought Harpreet wasn't good enough for me. This was the reason I never measured up to my beautiful, fair-skinned cousins!"

Naniji puts her hands on her hips. "Sharanjit, Harpreet showed his true colors shortly after your marriage, didn't he? We warned you, but you were too headstrong, and then you found yourself in a mess."

"But that's not why you didn't like him! No, Ma. You didn't

like him because he was too dark. And for you, being dark means something else . . . it means a lack of ambition, a flawed character, an *imperfection*, right?" Mom shoves her feet into her boots, grabs her coat, and charges out the door. I follow numbly behind.

"Sharan!" Uncle Sandeep calls, running after us.

Mom guns the engine, blasting cold air at us as I get into the car, shivering and pulling my coat tightly around myself. In the doorway, Nanaji and Naniji stand close together, faces pinched with something between shock and disappointment.

Uncle Sandeep jogs down the steps and taps on my window. I roll it down a couple of inches. "Sharan," he says across me to Mom. "Come on, don't run away again."

"Sandeep, I'm *tired* of this—not a thing has changed. It's hopeless." Her voice snags on "hopeless."

"Sharan, please . . ." He looks at her beseechingly.

"We're going, Sandeep," she says firmly, and throws the car into gear.

He looks defeated. "I'll call you soon," he says, stepping away.

I nod and whisper, "Bye."

As Mom screeches out of the driveway, I glance in the side mirror and see Uncle Sandeep climbing slowly back up the stairs to the front door. Naniji and Nanaji have closed the door and are standing together in the bay window, watching us drive away.

❖ ❖ ❖

All that waiting and wondering what it would be like to sit down to a meal with my family. We get out on the freeway and I want to cry and scream, or *something* . . . but I can't, because Mom beats me to it.

"I knew it was going to be a disaster!" she says, pounding the steering wheel. "I swore to myself I would never let it come to this, and here we are. I feel as if I never left that house!"

I can see her clenching and unclenching her jaw, while navigating the now darkening streets of New Jersey. It's just after five, and the sun has gone down, leaving behind a few solitary fingers of light.

"Sammy, I'm so sorry it had to be like this. Are you all right?"

I shrug. I honestly don't know what I am right now. I don't know if I'm all right—if I want to scream at her to shut up, or if I want to go back and scream at Naniji to shut up. No, actually, I would love it if Mom would shut up. I would love it if they all would just shut the hell up.

Mom's eyes are slits. She's clutching the steering wheel at the ten and two position, and she's sitting forward in her seat. "It's always been like this—since I was a child," she says. "My mother will *never* expand her views. I kept hoping and praying. I even asked Sandeep to make it abundantly clear that everyone keep their opinions about my marriage to themselves. *Especially* Ma."

"You brought it up," I say, leaning against the door and pulling my coat up around my chin.

"It was that photo. I'll bet she keeps it around to remind her how right she was. I wouldn't put it past her to have planted it there, just so she could rub my face in it."

"She had no idea I was going to ask to see pictures! And it's a good thing I did—I actually got to see what my own *father* looks like." I can't help the hard edge of bitterness that clings to my words.

She grips the steering wheel. "Sammy, I don't know how many different ways I can tell you this, but don't idealize your father. I assure you, he was anything but ideal. If he was, he would have come back around by now . . . at least to see *your* face, if not mine."

The sting I felt from her slap didn't hurt as much as this. I can't look at her, because looking at her might make me want to yell—or worse, cry. Words seem to be embedded into hardened concrete, deep inside my belly.

"Fine. He wasn't ideal," I finally manage. "But who is, Mom? No one is ideal enough for you. Nanaji and Naniji aren't ideal, you fight all the time with Uncle Sandeep. Mike wasn't ideal—"

"And look what that boy did!"

"Don't you see?" It escapes as a scream. "That's just what Naniji said! Didn't she say she 'warned' you about my father? And even if he turned out to be a jerk, you still had to find out for yourself, didn't you?"

"That's different," she says curtly.

"How is it different, Mom?" My voice cracks and I look out the window. Then I say quietly, "You know, you're not so ideal yourself."

In the reflection on the window, I see her turn sharply to look at me. But I keep staring out the window, watching the bare, leafless trees whiz by. They look naked and pitiful, like something out of a Robert Frost poem.

"Mom, you didn't even give them much of a chance. It was like you were expecting them to disappoint you. As soon as Naniji made a comment that confirmed your opinion, or fears, or whatever—you ran. You ran, Mom, not walked, you *ran* out the door! How can they 'expand their views' if you don't let them?" Mom has the steering wheel in a white-knuckled grip.

"How come it's all *them*? Don't you have anything that needs changing? Maybe you could expand *your* views or work *with* them on making changes."

"Sammy," she says, her voice sounding tight and controlled. "I grew up thinking that I was very unattractive because I was too dark, and that I was unacceptable precisely because of the kinds of references my mother made this afternoon.

"She would cluck to aunties and friends that I would be 'perfect, if only I hadn't been born so dark.' Most of them would subtly agree, though some would say something like, 'Oh, but she is bright, *nah*?' or 'Yes, but she is fine-featured.' I thought that nothing I did was enough, and that no matter how hard I tried, I would never measure up to what my mother wanted in a daughter. It took a real toll on my self-esteem, and it has taken many years to undo the damage."

She turns to me, her eyes spitting fire. "I don't want you to have to go through the same thing. And I'm afraid that if we have regular contact with them, you will. It's inevitable! Don't you see what I'm saying?"

No, I don't see. I don't care what you went through. You're not me. I'm not you. We ride the rest of the way home in a seething silence.

Chapter 16

Winter break has always been a lonely time for me. When I was little, Mom would fill it up with visits to friends' homes and a nice dinner for us. But it always fell short of the lively, glittering events I'd see on TV, and the ones I'd hear about from Molly, or at school from friends and classmates. This year is the worst it's ever been.

Inside our house feels like being in the eye of a hurricane. There's a huge storm raging all around, but where we are is silent, calm, deadly. Since any given moment could erupt in an explosion of sharp words, Mom and I maintain a tense civility between us.

I want to spend as much time with Molly as possible, but the MacFaddens are off on their yearly winter ski pilgrimage to Colorado. I'm actually relieved that it's almost over. At least when school starts, my days are full again. I've spent most of this break up in my room, catching up on schoolwork.

On Sunday the phone rings downstairs as I'm trying to solve a math problem. I race down to get it, thinking it might be Molly.

"Moll?"

"Samar!" It's Uncle Sandeep.

Tears spring to my eyes at the sound of his voice.

"Are you busy right now?" he asks.

"No."

"Have you had dinner?"

"Yeah, Mom made snapper."

"Where is she?"

I look around for a note. There's one on the kitchen table: *Sammy, stepping out for a couple of hours.* Maybe she went for another session with Tina the therapist. Ever since we came back from Nanaji and Naniji's, Mom's been seeing Tina regularly.

"She stepped out for a bit."

"How about I take you out for tea?"

"Yes!"

"I'll be there in ten minutes."

I scribble a note for Mom and rush upstairs to change. I'm so thrilled to see him when he rolls up that I almost pull a Mom and run out of the house in my socks. When I get into the car, it smells like incense and basmati rice, and he has Punjabi folk music playing.

I throw my arms around him. "Hi, Uncle Sandeep!"

"Samar, it's wonderful to see you again too," he says with a laugh. Then, more seriously, "How is Sharan?"

"You know Mom."

He nods and squints. "Don't be too hard on her, Samar. That was a very difficult and emotional meeting for all of us. Things like this take time . . . it was a first step."

"Whatever. She's always right, and she's *so* perfect. I don't know how you put up with her for so many years."

"She's also kind, fiercely loyal, and loving. Maybe even to a fault."

"Yeah, her love is like a boa constrictor. That kind of love I could do without."

He pulls into Teas Me and we run in, bracing ourselves against the cold. I grab a table, and Uncle Sandeep comes back with a pot of chai tea.

"So," he says, dropping into a plush, overstuffed chair across from me.

"So."

"Tell me."

"I don't know," I say, watching him pour tea into mugs. I think back to the day of our visit and involuntarily tense up. "It was . . ." I stop to take a deep breath.

He nods encouragingly.

"Mom and I had a huge fight in the car on the way back."

He wrinkles his eyebrows and leans back to take a sip.

"It was about my father."

He stops sipping and sets his mug down. "I thought that might come up."

"Mom never showed me any pictures of him, ever! That was the first picture I've ever seen, and now I see where I get my cheekbones, and . . ." I get choked up and stop.

"Go on."

"Why didn't she at least show me a picture?" I ask through pools of tears.

He warms one hand against his mug. "Samar . . . I know it must be difficult for you to understand." He shakes his head. "But Sharan was doing what she thought best at the time. Just as she thought keeping you from our parents would protect you, so she thought about Harpreet."

"She says I shouldn't idealize him." A thought suddenly flashes through my head. "Wait. *You* knew him, right?"

He gives a reluctant nod and picks up his mug.

"What . . . what was he like?"

Uncle Sandeep takes a long sip of his tea. Then he sets his mug down and looks thoughtful for several moments before he answers. "Harpreet was a very intelligent fellow." He looks over my shoulder and out the window, as if the words are somewhere in the darkness outside. "He was charming and suave. Your mother fell hard and fast for him . . . many girls did. He was very likeable. Had a great sense of humor."

I fold my hands tightly, lacing the fingers together, and shove them between the warmth of my thighs. I savor the words he drops, like forbidden treats.

He looks directly into my eyes. "Your mother is right, though, Samar. You should not idealize him. Sharan thought that being with him would get her away from our parents—which it did—but she wasn't any happier." He picks up his mug again.

I want more. I need to know more about this man that my mother has kept away from me. "But he sounds fantastic! Why would she need to protect me from someone like that?"

He looks up at the ceiling. "Samar, you really should have this discussion with your mother."

"I *have*. She doesn't tell me *anything*, Uncle Sandeep."

He sits up again and heaves a deep sigh. "She discovered that he had been having a relationship with one of his coworkers. And apparently, he had taken you with him to one of their rendezvous sites. Sharan had some sort of inner sense, or 'women's intuition,' and she followed him one weekend when he said he was taking you out for ice cream. Which he did, only the other woman was with him."

I'm leaning forward in my seat, waiting anxiously for him to continue. I have no recollection of any of what Uncle Sandeep has just told me, but it's hard to imagine someone doing something like that to Mom, never mind the fact that she got into her car and *followed* my father. It's like something out of a bad movie.

"Samar, are you all right?" he asks gently.

I swallow hard and nod. "So, what happened?"

He continues, though a bit uncertainly. "She immediately moved the two of you out into an apartment on the other side of town and filed for a divorce. Of course, divorce being the ugly, stinking boil of stigma that it is in our culture, Harpreet's parents were nothing short of hostile toward her. They tried very hard to convince her to accept what he had done and 'work it out,' for your sake, Samar."

He pauses for a moment before continuing. "It became very messy and ugly between the families, each accusing the other of soiling their reputation and family honor.

"Both sides," he says, shaking his head, "put tremendous pressure on Sharan to stay in the marriage and turn a blind eye to Harpreet's betrayal. Even Ma and Papa, who didn't like Harpreet from the beginning, didn't want the shame of a divorce to muddy the pristine Ahluwahlia reputation. Their stance was, 'You made your bed, now go and lie in it.' But Sharan wouldn't even entertain the thought. Good thing, too, because within a year of the divorce being finalized, Harpreet had married that same lady friend in a large and lavish wedding that was the talk of the whole community for months."

I remember Mom's comment about my father after we left Naniji and Nanaji's house: *He was anything but ideal. If he was, he would have come back around by now . . . at least to see your face, if not mine.*

Of course. The comment had stung then, but it made sense now. Why would he come back around if he had a whole new life, possibly with other children, even?

To see me, came a faint whisper from somewhere way down inside.

But he hadn't.

I wrap my hands around my mug, more to keep them from trembling than anything else.

"Can you see why she wouldn't readily share this with you, Samar?"

I nod. If Mom had told me this when I was little, I don't know how I would've handled it. Especially since I'm not doing such a great job with it now.

"She was doing her best."

I nod again, deep in my own thoughts as this piece of information slips through the layers of time and fits with other pieces to give me a bigger picture of how the moments in my life come together.

"It's amazing how one single event can change everything," I say slowly. "Forever."

He reaches across to cup my face in one hand. "Your mother is an exceptional woman, Samar," he says with a wink. "And she has raised an exceptional daughter."

I smile wanly. "Even if I am a coconut."

He wrinkles his eyebrows in confusion. "Hmm?"

I lean back in my chair and sigh. "Before we went to visit Naniji and Nanaji, I was worried that they would think I was a coconut. One of the Indian girls at school called me that."

"How is that an insult?" he asks with a puzzled look.

"It means that you're brown on the outside and white on the inside. It means you don't know who you really are."

Understanding dawns in his eyes. "Ahhh," he says with a nod. Then he jabs a finger into the air between us. "But the coconut is also a symbol of resilience, Samar. Even in conditions where there's very little nourishment and even less nurturance, it flourishes, growing taller than most of the plants around it."

Intrigued, I get ready to ask more about coconuts and flourishing and resilience. I want to know more about Mom and what makes her exceptional. More about Harpreet and how he and Mom met, and all the years leading up to when Mom stopped talking to her family for good. But Uncle Sandeep's cell phone buzzes, then rings.

"Just a minute—that might be Sharan," he says, flipping it open.

"Blocked ID." He closes it and puts it back into his pocket. Right away, it buzzes again. He knits his brow as he looks at the caller ID.

He holds up a finger. "One second, Samar . . . Hello?"

I sit back and sigh. I know there's no rush. I have plenty of time to ask Uncle Sandeep to fill me in on everything Mom left out all these years.

His eyes widen in alarm as he scrambles to his feet. He speaks rapidly in Punjabi as he grabs his coat and belongings. *Naniji and Nanaji!* I quickly grab my things and follow. He clicks off his phone as we rush out of the tea shop.

"Is it Naniji and Nanaji?" I ask, buckling myself into the seat.

"No," he says, his voice strained. "It's the gurdwara—the temple I took you to. Someone has thrown a makeshift bomb through one of the windows."

My heart pounds a furious drumbeat in my ears on the way to the gurdwara. I clutch the door handle as Uncle Sandeep speeds all the way there.

A makeshift bomb.

When we round the corner and the gurdwara comes into view, my hand flies to my chest as I let out a choked gasp.

The gurdwara is burning. The place where I had those moments of complete serenity is now swallowed by flames. They leap like dancers, red and yellow arms stabbing into the night sky, embers flying, and sparks disappearing into the stars.

Uncle Sandeep leaves me with a frail old woman standing in the cold in her slippers and runs into the burning building. I try to run in after him, but the woman's grip is solid. She shakes her head and speaks to me in Punjabi. I take my scarf and hat and offer them to her. She nods gratefully, blessing me with her hand on my head, just as Nanaji had done.

Uncle Sandeep stumbles out, carrying an unconscious young man. He deposits him by an open van where people huddle together, staring at the inferno before them, then runs back inside. I call to him, but he doesn't hear me. I lead the old woman to the van, where we huddle close, next to the others.

When Uncle Sandeep comes back outside, minutes later, the fire has spread to the other side of the building. He has his arm around an old man, leading him away from the danger. I recognize the old man as the one who was reading the Holy Book the day that I was here. A day that seems so long ago now.

Uncle Sandeep takes his coat and hands it to the old man, whose own clothes are hanging off him, charred and torn in places.

He turns to look at the building disintegrating before our eyes. He walks slowly to where I sit with the old woman and drops to his knees next to us. Shadows of flames leap on his face, but the real fire is in his eyes. He clenches his hands into fists and places them against his temples, then lowers his head to look down at the ground.

Soon the firefighters arrive and begin to shout instructions and commands all around us. Snowflakes dance and fall while a numbing cold seeps into me. *How could this happen?*

I look up at the fluffy snowflakes swirling against the night sky and lean my head against Uncle Sandeep. He puts his arm around me, and the faint scent of coconut oil mingles with the smell of burning wood and smoke.

"Samar, I'm calling your mother to pick you up. I need to stay here and help." As the firefighters gain control, he reaches for his cell phone and dials. "Sharan, it's Sandeep. I'm here with Samar at the gurdwara—it's burning. Yes, yes, she's fine. Yes, okay."

He turns to me. "She's on her way," he says, leading me back to the car. He gets in and turns the heat up. "You need to go home," he says quietly.

"I want to stay."

He shakes his head. "No, Samar. It's much better for you to go home. School tomorrow, no?"

I stand my ground. "I want to help . . . I want to do *something*."

He looks me in the eyes. There is deep sadness in the creases of his face, but a firm resoluteness in his voice. "Absolutely," he says. "You *must* do something. But for tonight, the best thing you can do is go home and get ready for school."

"But . . ." My breath snags in my chest and the rest of the sentence is swallowed by a strangled sob. My chin trembles as I try to keep myself together.

"I will sit with you until Sharan arrives," he says, kindly but irrefutably, and lapses into silence.

We watch the firefighters work, putting warm wraps around the members of the gurdwara and offering words of comfort. Uncle Sandeep leans back and looks through his sunroof at the fingernail moon.

"Do you remember that Winnie the Pooh blanket I gave you?"

I nod, wiping my tears with the back of my hand. "I still have it."

He continues to stare out the sunroof. "Do you know why I gave it to you?" He doesn't wait for an answer. "You were my *muni* . . . that's an affectionate nickname for little girls." He pauses for a moment. "I liked that nickname for you because it also sounded like the English word 'moon.' My moon-y."

He turns to look at me with a sad smile. "You were like the moon when you were a child, Samar. You would look up at the faces of the adults around you and absorb, absorb, absorb." He waves the air toward his face as if waving a scent toward his nose. "You absorbed everything you heard and saw and reflected it back in its entirety, just as the moon absorbs the sun's rays all day and reflects them back at night." He stops to rub his eyes with two fingers.

"You were the first child I had ever been that close to," he continues. "I was completely disarmed by your innocence and your heart, with its doors flung wide open." His eyes shimmer as he looks back up at the moon. "That is why I had to come back. I missed Sharan terribly, but I also missed my *muni*."

He looks at me again. "Children are little bundles of love, Samar. We were all children once. We all started out that way . . . sleeping peacefully like my little *muni*, with her Winnie the Pooh stars and moon blanket." He swallows hard, his Adam's apple bobbing above his shirt collar.

Headlights pierce the darkness around us. A car door slams, and Mom's voice slices through the night. "Sammy! Sandeep!"

"We're here!" he says, stepping out of the car. He hugs

Mom tightly. "Take Samar home, Sharan. I'll stay to make sure everyone is all right."

Mom give his hand a quick squeeze, then puts an arm firmly around me and steers me to her car. I lean my head on her shoulder and look back at Uncle Sandeep as he walks toward the firefighters.

Chapter 17

Mom spent most of the night up with me, making hot chocolate, crooning in my ear, telling me everything would be okay, until I finally passed out. This morning my lack of sleep is clearly evident under my eyes.

"Wally, you look like crap," Molly says as soon as she sees my face.

"Thanks."

"What happened?" She bangs her locker shut and gives the combination lock a whirl. We start walking to first period calculus. I'm grateful today's not a quiz day.

"You remember the temple my uncle took me to?" She nods. "Last night someone threw a makeshift bomb through one of the windows. The whole place went up in flames."

She stops walking and stares at me. "The temple?" she breathes, dumbfounded. She shakes her head as if she doesn't believe what I'm saying. "I mean, throwing stuff at a passing car is one thing, but setting a temple where people pray on fire?"

"I know. . . ." I stop before the words dissolve into tears.

We walk to the most secluded bathroom in the school. She

sets her books down on the window ledge, taking mine from me as well. I perch on the edge of one of the sinks. She puts her hands against the wall and leans her forehead between them.

"Sammy . . . I don't even know what to say." Her voice is soft and quivery.

I lean my head back against the mirror. "It's not your fault."

She turns around, this time leaning her back against the wall, and slides to the floor. "No, this isn't," she says, raking her hands through her hair and holding it back with both hands. "But I've been doing a lot of thinking."

I raise my eyebrows, waiting for her to finish.

"That day that Uncle Sandeep first came to my house . . . you know, it was Great-Aunt Maggie's birthday . . ."

I nod slowly.

"You were right, Wally. There was a weird vibe going on. I felt it, I just . . . I didn't know what to do about it." She brings her hands into her lap and stares at them. "My parents, hell, my whole family, *loves* you! And . . . and Uncle Sandeep is the *best*."

I hop off the sink and slide down next to her. She's talking so quietly, I have to lean close to hear what she's saying. "Everything's so messed up, Wally."

"Yeah, it is," I say softly.

The warning bell rings. She pushes herself up onto her feet. "You okay?"

I shrug. "You?"

She shrugs. "Let's get to class. The last thing we need right now is school stress."

We grab our books and head out. Before I open the door, I turn around. "Hey, Moll?"

"Yeah?"

"Thanks."

She gives me a shaky smile. "BFF?"

I nod. "Definitely."

When we walk into Lim's class, I feel just a tiny bit lighter. Like getting through the day won't be as hard as it seemed when I first walked into the school.

During English, Lesiak crams class time with Fitzgerald's statement about the disintegration of the American Dream in *The Great Gatsby*. "It may seem like a book about a love story gone awry, but Fitzgerald was making a stinging commentary about the decaying social and moral values of his time." I try to focus, but it's like using a sieve to fill a bucket.

After class, I gather my books and look around for Balvir, but she's already left. I've begun to look forward to our lunchtime chats. When I walk out into the hall, I see her standing a few feet from the English room, chatting with Shazia Azem. When she sees me, Balvir motions me over.

I hadn't noticed it before, but as I walk toward them, I notice the dark circles under Balvir's eyes and the redness around her nose.

"Hey, Sammy," she says weakly. "I've asked Shazia to hang out with us during lunch."

"Cool," I say, nodding to Shazia.

It's an unusually warm day for January, with the temperature somewhere in the sixties. One of the only possible perks of global warming. When the three of us get to "our" tree, Balvir's words pour out, like a faucet suddenly turning on. "Sammy, I was just telling Shazia that the temple I go to with my family was set on fire yesterday."

I whip my head around. It had never occurred to me that she would go to the same gurdwara as Uncle Sandeep, but of course she would. How many gurdwaras could there be in this area? I swallow hard and stare at her.

Her face is tight. "I wasn't there, but my grandmother was. She said a window was smashed and a burning ball came flying through. It hit the drapes and they burned straight up to the ceiling."

Shazia shakes her head. "I'm so sorry, Balvir. It's amazing that whenever there's social or political unrest, it's the churches, synagogues, and temples that get targeted first."

"But why?" I whisper. "Why those places?"

She sighs and shakes her head again. "I don't know. . . ."

Balvir continues as if she hasn't heard a word. "What is wrong with people?" she demands, her eyes becoming teary. "Sikhs are not Muslims!" She turns quickly to Shazia and says, "No offense."

Then she continues, spitting words like a machine gun. "Sikhism has only been around for the last five centuries, with over twenty *million* followers in the world! It has nothing to do with Islam." She wraps her arms around her bent knees, her back expanding and contracting with deep sobs.

I stroke her back and quickly brush my own tears aside. For some reason, I don't want her to know that I was there. Her grief, and mine, feels private. She may be sharing with me and Shazia, but it's more like a pressure valve, releasing just a tiny bit of steam off the top, so that she can go on with her day. I wonder if she had someone who crooned into her ear all night and brought her hot chocolate. Or if she has a BFF who would drag her into a remote bathroom for a BFF chat, just to let her know she's not alone.

After a lengthy pause, Shazia clears her throat. "Balvir, you want to distinguish between Sikhs and Muslims because of . . . what? Do you think that the violence will be less if you do?" Balvir looks up at her.

Shazia shifts uneasily but continues. "Please don't be upset by my saying this, but if you think *your* family is targeted, imagine my brothers, Khaled and Ahmed." She looks down at the grass.

Balvir has calmed down, like the pressure is now at a manageable level. She rubs her face with both hands. "You're right, Shazia. Of course, I know you're right." She turns to me. "Sammy, Shazia is a couple of years older than us. She moved here from the Middle East last summer."

"The UAE—United Arab Emirates," Shazia clarifies. "It hasn't been easy being a Muslim in America after the attacks either, believe me. I don't wear a scarf, but some of my cousins do, and they've been getting harassed almost daily where they live. It's unreal, you know . . . especially since Islam is such a religion of peace."

Balvir gives Shazia an affectionate nudge. "She's supposed to be in college already, but they put her back because the school system is different there. She sure seems to know a hell of a lot more than the rest of us."

Shazia gives me a smile and extends her hand. "We got different news coverage there. I have a very different take on America and world events because of it."

I shake her hand, something I'm not accustomed to doing with other seniors. "It's nice to formally meet you."

We eat our lunches in silence for a few minutes. When I finish mine, I turn to Balvir. "Is your grandmother okay?"

She nods. "She's fine, just a little freaked out. Not everyone was as lucky as she was, though."

I nod and allow the silence to settle on us again. There are so many different kinds of silence. The kind I've had with Mom: silence when it came to my father and grandparents; silence about Indian-ness and anything that might set me apart from my American counterparts; and the "treatment" kind, when I've done something she disapproves of. Then there are the silences I had with Mike: silence about who I am—because, to be fair, I didn't really know myself; silence about things he said or did . . . or *watched*, that made me squirm, but I had no idea why. And then there's the silence at the gurdwara that made me turn inward and discover that the world inside is as vast as the world outside.

Sitting next to Balvir gives me the strangest feeling. We have so much in common, and yet at the same time we have nothing in common. I sit still and close my eyes. This silence now is a different kind of silence. It's the silence that comes after running and running and running, and then turning a corner.

❖ ❖ ❖

At the end of the day, Molly and Bobbi meet me at my locker.

"Ready?" Molly asks.

I nod and heave my backpack onto my shoulder as we start walking.

Bobbi starts in right away. "So the Midwinter Dance committee met again today. I think it's going to be an amazing dance. You're both coming, right?"

Molly says, "Sure," while I give a half nod, half shrug.

"The music is gonna be banging," she continues. "We've booked DJ Funkalicious already!"

"Wow, she's hard to book," Molly says, impressed.

Bobbi looks pleased. "Not when you have connections."

I roll my eyes, out of her line of vision.

Bobbi continues, "Have you decided what you're going to wear? I think I'm going to do the glittery jeans thing. . . ."

I tune out as they discuss the dance. I can't stop last night from replaying in my mind: Uncle Sandeep telling me about my father; the gurdwara walls blackening in flames; the fingernail moon shining through the sunroof; sleeping *muni* with her Winnie the Pooh stars and moon blanket . . . *me*, with my yum-yum.

"Sammy? You still with us?"

I pull myself together and look at Bobbi. "Sorry, what did you say?"

"Is your ex still harassing you?"

I shake my head. "Haven't heard from him since Mom talked to Mrs. B."

She smiles. "Funny how much influence a boy's mama can have."

❖ ❖ ❖

When I get home, Mom's at the kitchen table sorting bills. She looks up as I walk through the door. "Hi, honey. How are you doing?"

I shrug. "Okay, I guess." I get out of my winter gear and sit down next to her. "Guess it's a little much."

She nods, folding her hands in front of her and resting her chin on top. "I'm glad you weren't hurt. At first I thought Sandeep had taken you to the gurdwara again. I don't know what I would've done if . . ." She takes a breath and stops to stroke my upper arm.

I look at her face, brimming with concern, fear, and . . . relief. At one time a comment like that might've made me feel smothered. But now I take her hand and hold it between mine. We're almost the exact same shade of brown, the color of warm maple syrup and cinnamon over waffles.

"I'm okay, Mom," I say softly.

She slides her hand out and cups my face before planting a big, sloppy kiss on my mouth. She grins, still holding on to my face. "Remember when I used to give you puppy kisses?"

I yank my head away before she can lick the entire length of my face. "Ewww, Mom!"

She laughs. "Don't worry, that was before acne and gym class." She looks back down at her bills. "A lot of homework tonight?"

"Yeah," I say, not making a move to go upstairs.

She looks up after a moment, eyebrows raised. "Something else?"

"About Naniji and Nanaji."

She stiffens but waits quietly.

"Mom, don't you think that grandparents, in general, are just set in their ways? Like, they *might* change their views, but most likely they won't, because they grew up a certain way during a certain time and that's when they got set in their beliefs?"

Mom sets her pen down gently but firmly. She sighs before looking up again at me. "That's true, Sammy," she says. "Most older adults aren't likely to change their worldviews as readily as younger adults. But the issues I have with my parents are more than simply age-related. Valuing lighter complexions runs across the board in Indian culture. It's not just my parents, it's really a phenomenon . . . and it usually goes hand in hand with valuing materialism, social status, and a whole host of other things that I've spent years teaching you to challenge."

"Well maybe that's the point," I say, choosing my words carefully. "That it's *not* just your parents. And the light-skin, materialism values are more of a cultural thing. Maybe everything you've been trying to teach me about is something that's not only about Naniji and Nanaji, but a lot bigger."

She chews on her bottom lip. The faintest hint of doubt flits like a shadow across her face. After a moment, she looks into my eyes. "You may be right," she says slowly. "I wanted my parents to challenge the way things were, not accept them. I *needed* that from them . . . and I might have felt that they failed me by not doing that." She runs her finger along the edge of an envelope.

"My mother, especially," she continues. "I suppose I expected more from her because she was the same gender parent." She looks out the window, as if lost in a memory. "I kept them away from you because I was afraid they would fail you in some way, the way they failed me. I couldn't bear the thought of you feeling that same sense of betrayal."

"They couldn't fail me the same way. They're not my parents; *you* are . . . and you've never failed me that way."

She looks at me as if she's focusing on my features for the very first time. "Huh," she says, like an answer to a deeply perplexing, long-held riddle finally surfaces in her head.

"Yes, *I* am your mother." She shakes her head and mumbles, "Come to think of it, I was probably protecting *myself* more than anyone else by keeping us both away from my parents." She continues to shake her head, lost in her own thoughts. "I guess we're most blind to our own issues."

After a long and silent pause where we're both contemplating different things on our own little islands, she sighs deeply.

I snap my head up.

She looks at me for a long moment, and a look of extreme satisfaction creeps onto her face. She nods once and says, "I have to finish these bills, Sammy-beans."

Chapter 18

Two weeks go by pretty fast when you've got quizzes and papers coming out the wazoo. I don't know what these teachers think they're preparing us for, but I've become one homework machine. By the time Bobbi's Midwinter Dance rolls around, I am ready to party.

After much pleading and promising to be home by midnight, Molly manages to snag her parents' car for the evening. I hear her bouncing up the stairs before she swooshes into my room and grabs my arm.

"Diego said he'll be there a bit later with Ajay," she says. She's been jittery ever since she decided that Diego was the Real Deal. "You know that Ajay's father is Nigerian and his mother's from Bangladesh?"

I roll my eyes. "Please, Moll. I've had enough guy drama for a while."

She drops my arm. "Sorry, just thought I'd mention it."

I look at her closely. "So . . . is tonight the night?"

"I don't know!" She squeezes my forearm, leaving fading

yellow fingerprints behind. "What if it is? God! Makes me so nervous I can't even think straight!"

I wriggle into my black jeans and suck my gut in to pull up the zipper.

I give Molly an appreciative glance. She has on fuzzy tights and a skintight leopard-skin dress. "Wow, cashmere and animal print—*looove* it. Only you could pull that off, Moll. Nobody else could make fuzzy kitty look sexy." I slip a stretchy black lace V-neck over my head.

"Talk about sexy, Wally."

I look at my reflection in the mirror. "Well, thaink ya."

"We are gonna knock 'em on their asses tonight."

I slide Diva Red across my lips before we head for the door. Mom's on the couch, watching *As Good as It Gets* on DVD for the third time.

"Bye, Mom." I leave a Diva Red mouth print on her cheek.

"Have fun, girls! Don't do anything I wouldn't do."

"We promise," Molly says merrily.

Once in the car, Molly blasts the music as loud as we can handle. When we pull into the school lot, people are slowly trickling in.

"Can I leave my bag in here?" I ask, pulling my lipstick out.

"Sure, I'll leave mine, too. We can put them in the trunk."

We throw our bags in the back and walk into the gym.

DJ Funkalicious is set up at the front with a dry ice machine next to her. There are two disco balls spraying diamond-shaped lights all over the floor. We drop our jackets behind the DJ booth. Molly was right, knowing Bobbi Lewis does have some perks.

"Let's dance!" I yell, pulling Molly onto the dance floor. Several people are already there, and Molly and I join them.

The music thrums through my spiky-heeled boots and straight up my legs. The songs meld together into one throbbing beat. It's just me and the vibrations from the floor, the flashing lights, and the occasional clouds of dry ice. Before I know it, I'm in the middle of a huge throng of people.

I feel warm inside and out. Bodies rub and bump against me from all sides. Everyone knows that being in the middle of the dance floor almost guarantees you'll get felt up. If you don't want it, stay on the outskirts, where the chaperones can keep an eye on things.

I stay put. I like the heat, the pulsing of rhythms, breath, and limbs all around me. It's the perfect place to submerge and zone out. Exactly what I need.

When Funkalicious slows down the pace, I realize how parched I am. I walk over to the DJ booth and lean against the wall to scour the room for Molly. I find her, superglued to Diego, barely moving in time to the slow song. Next to them is Diego's friend, Ajay.

I look him over with some interest. Not bad, not bad at all. But not now. The space that Mike left behind is still raw and jumbled. I need time to sort that out before I venture back out onto the guy minefield.

I sigh and head toward the door. Outside the gym, fluorescent lights beam daytime into the halls. Students line up against the window ledge, looking out onto the courtyard, chatting and flirting. I walk straight to the water fountain and suck until the person behind me starts to complain.

"Hey, leave some for the rest of us!"

I roll my eyes, take a few more gulps, and turn to go back into the gym. The slow song is still playing, so I lean against the DJ booth where it's darkest and pretend to go through my jacket pockets in search of something.

Finally the pace picks up with a Puffy-turned-P. Diddy tune. I take a couple of steps toward the dance floor, then stop to stare at the gym entrance.

There's Mike, sauntering in like he still goes here. Star of Melville High. He's followed by the Three Jerk-a-teers—Rick Taylor, Simon Monroe, Chuck Banfield—and a couple of guys I don't recognize. My heart quickens as I look away. I sidle up to Molly, who's now got at least an inch between herself and Diego.

"Moll . . ." I lean in close to be heard above the bass.

She turns to me, eyes blissfully glazed. "Hey, Sammy!"

I shout into her ear. "Mike just walked in!" Her expression changes in an instant and she looks around, disentangling from Mr. Real Deal.

When she spots Mike, her face hardens. "Don't worry, Sam. He wouldn't do anything here."

I nod and do a two-step next to her. A few minutes later Bobbi prances over with a couple of her sidekicks. "I just saw Mr. X," she says, shouting into my ear. "Are you all right?"

I nod and keep dancing. We're pretty close to the outer edge of the dance floor, so I know Mike has spotted me, but I avoid looking in the direction where he and his friends have set up camp.

After a while, I almost loosen up a little. When Funkalicious slows down the tempo again, I walk to the back near the booth. I see Martin Shaheen grab Bobbi's hand just as she's reaching for her cup of water, and her sidekicks are already plastered against guys. Molly's snuggled up against Diego, but she throws me an apologetic look over her shoulder.

I pick up my coat to start my searching-through-the-pockets routine, when I see Ajay walking toward me. I toss my coat aside in relief and get ready to go out on the dance floor. But before Ajay makes it anywhere close, Mike steps in front of him.

"Hey, Sammy." My heart leaps into my throat.

Ajay stops and leans against the wall.

In a flash, Molly is at my side, hands on hips. "Buzz off, creep!" Diego and Ajay have come together and now hover nearby, watching closely.

"If there's a problem, I'll have security over here in ten seconds flat," Molly says.

Bobbi and her sidekicks have found a prime viewing spot off to one side.

"Relax," Mike says sharply. "This is between me and Sammy." He looks directly at me. "Sammy, can we *please* talk? Just for a sec?"

In that moment, something in his eyes reminds me of the Mike I fell for: the Mike in high school who used to be happy, before he had to start working full-time and taking care of his mom; the Mike who loved to draw and laugh and drive to the lake. The Mike who saw lots of possibility for himself in the world and thought it was a good place. I can tell he's not drunk, and my insides begin to mush up.

"It's okay," I say to Molly.

"Are you sure?" says Molly, looking suspiciously at Mike, then over his shoulder at the guys he came in with.

I nod. "I won't leave the building."

She walks away slowly, casting looks back at me as she makes her way to Diego and Ajay.

"Good friend," he says to me.

I slide down onto our heap of jackets. "What do you want, Mike?"

He crouches down in front of me. "I miss you, Sam."

"Shoulda thought of that before you left those messages on my voice mail." We're still yelling over the music.

"Yeah, about that." He looks around the room. "Can we go somewhere quieter?"

I look at him like, *Why should I?*

"I'm sorry!" he says.

I chew on my bottom lip for a minute. What the hell. We could go out into the hallway where everything's lit up like a stadium. I get up. He holds his hand out, but I ignore it and walk past him. We go to a spot that's relatively vacant and lean against the window ledge.

"Listen," he says, prying open a window. "I'm sorry about being an asswipe. There's no excuse for what I said and how I acted. I was way outta line."

I take a deep breath in. Being this warm, having just left a room that was throbbing with music and bodies, then standing this close to Mike, is not easy. And he knows it.

He takes my hand and traces the lines on it before bringing it to his lips. His mouth lightly grazes the center of my palm, warm breath radiating to my fingertips and up my arms.

I jerk my hand away. "Cut it out, Mike."

He flashes a lopsided smile. The one that makes me forget how to form words into sentences. He tilts his head to give me a once-over. "You look great, Sam."

I can't help the tremor that races through my body. At one time I thought Mike would be my Real Deal. And even though every inch of me wants to plaster up against him on the dance floor, those voice mail messages keep replaying in my head.

I turn toward the gym entrance. "I'm going back in."

He grabs my hand again. "C'mon, Sam."

"See you later, Mike," I say softly, and pull my hand out of his.

I feel like a pinball in a machine as I walk back through the crowd, not only because I'm being jostled, but because of the million thoughts pinging through my brain. The place is packed now, and almost everyone is dancing. Molly has melted back into Diego in a darkened part of the room. I glance at the giant wall clock, and it is in its usual broken state. I reach for my cell to check the time and remember that I left it in my bag in the trunk of the MacFaddens' car. Given Molly's swoony state, I figure I should probably be the one to keep an eye on the time.

I weave my way toward her and lightly tap her shoulder. "Hey, Moll—sorry, Diego—I need to get my bag out of the car!"

She fishes her keys out of a pocket, still mostly melded to

Diego. I take them, stop by the booth for my jacket, and walk out to the parking lot.

It's freezing out now, and I'm wishing I had decided on flannels and fleece. The parking lot is dark, shadowy, and deserted, except for a group of guys hanging out near a red Ford Mustang. I quicken my pace as I walk past them.

I snatch my bag out of the trunk and shove my phone into my jacket pocket. I slam the trunk shut and start walking back to the building.

As I walk past the Mustang, I notice that the voices have died down. I hear shuffling and the clinking of bottles. And then a figure steps in front of me.

"Look who it is."

My blood runs cold as Chuck's voice slivers into me. I can't see his face because of the light behind him. He sways in front of me, holding a bottle in a paper bag. He reeks of booze.

"Buzz off, Banfield," I mutter. I turn to walk around him and slam into Simon.

Simon moves toward me and I back away. "Saw you dancing in there, Ali-ali-ali," he says, moving toward me. "Looked to me like you like being rubbed up."

Blood pounds in my ears. They're standing between me and the entrance to the building. There doesn't seem to be a soul in sight. I put my hands in the pockets of my jacket and grip my cell phone. I wonder if I could hit Molly's number by randomly pressing keys. No, they'll hear the beeps.

Rick's voice comes out of the shadows to my right. I gasp and take a step back. "Remember when we used to chase you in the schoolyard, Ali-ali?" He starts laughing. "Hey, Chuck, remember when you put that worm on Ali-ali's head?"

Chuck laughs.

My throat is closing. A storm swirls in my belly.

His voice is smooth, his breath coming out in puffs laced with alcohol. "I got somethin' else for ya, and it ain't no worm."

"Yeah," says Simon, moving closer. "Let's see what's got Mike all worked up."

I edge farther back. *Think, think, think, Sammy!* Behind me are trees and hedges. If I scream, no one will hear me above the music inside.

No sudden movements. I take a deep breath, twitch my head to look over Chuck's shoulder, at a point on the brick school wall behind him. Then I yell as loud as I can, "Mike!"

The three of them jerk their heads around, and I bolt in the opposite direction. Mom told me that in third grade when I came home muddy and bruised: *If you can't outfight them, baby, RUN.*

And I run. I don't stop to look back. I don't feel the cold. I don't feel my nose dripping. I don't feel my toes pinched in pointy, spike-heeled boots. I don't feel nausea.

I feel wind and fire. I run down the hill and into a thicket of bushes. I dive in, away from any light, and crouch in the darkness. I wait. My breathing is too loud. I'm shivering so hard my teeth hammer together inside my mouth. I watch and I wait like a cornered mouse, but no one follows me.

I don't know how long I sit there, squatting in the bushes in the dark, but my fingers go numb and my ears feel like they'll fall off. I blow on my hands and pull out my cell phone. Molly? No, she won't hear her phone.

I force my stiff fingers to dial Mom. It rings through to voice mail. I shove my hands under my armpits to keep them warm. I try Mom again, and again get the voice mail. A sob escapes from deep down.

Where the hell are you, Mom?

I dial Uncle Sandeep. Halfway through the first ring, he picks up. "Samar?"

My teeth chatter and I'm shivering so hard, I'm almost convulsing. "U-u-uncle San-san-deep . . ."

"Samar! What's wrong?" His voice rings with alarm. "Where are you?"

"S-s-school . . . dance . . . Roose-v-velt Ave . . ."

"Don't *move*. I'll be there in a few minutes."

I pull my collar up around my neck and shove my hands into my pockets. My fingers wrap around my phone, holding it tight.

I wait. Each minute feels like an eternity. Several cars drive past, and I peer out of my hiding spot to see if any slow down. Finally I see a set of headlights driving slower than the other cars that have gone by. As the car draws nearer, I see the sea-green of his Buick Regal, and the forest green of his turban inside. I stagger out.

"Samar!" He stops the car, jumps out, and runs to help me in. I'm so frozen, I can barely move. I sit down, shrinking into a fetal position.

He blasts the heat, then pulls me close. "Samar, tell me what happened!" His words are punctuated with panic. He rocks me until my fingers begin to move again. Bit by bit, I thaw and uncurl.

"Shall we go to the police? Did someone hurt you?" He slams a fist onto the steering wheel.

I shake my head and look out the window. In the reflection, I see a puffy face with scratches, a crusty nose, and smudges of dirt. "Those guys who threw stuff at your car . . . ," I begin. "They were in the parking lot, and—and I needed to get something from the car, and . . ." I stop to reach up and wipe a tear away.

I hear a sharp intake of breath next to me. Uncle Sandeep cups my face, staring at the scratches and dirt on my cheeks. "Those boys!" Then, through clenched teeth, "*Enough. Something must be done!*"

Before I can say anything more, Uncle Sandeep is out of the car and racing toward the school.

"Wait!" I shout, but he doesn't hear me.

I cut the engine, stuff the keys into my pocket, and scramble out. Uncle Sandeep is out of my line of vision, but I scuttle through the bushes, around the fence, and back up the hill. As I near the parking lot, I hear loud voices around the corner. Two of them are clearly Chuck Banfield and Rick Taylor.

Rivers of cold dread pump through my veins as I will my legs to move faster. The voices get louder.

Just before I turn the corner into the parking lot, I hear the squeal of tires and a sickening thud. I freeze for a moment as every system in my body shuts down. Then, just as quickly, adrenaline shoots through my limbs, and I sprint around the corner.

I see a red Ford Mustang careening out of the parking lot.

Everything else moves in slow, liquid motion. I see it all happening from above, like I'm floating up in the night sky. The doors of the school are flung open and several people run out. A chaperone shouts for someone to call 911.

I see myself moving dazedly toward a crumpled heap of clothes on the ground as a crowd begins to gather. I see my hand reaching out to straighten a forest green turban as it waves in the wind, like a flag.

Chapter 19

'm in the ambulance, holding tight to Uncle Sandeep's hand. Somewhere in the distance, I hear the words of the EMS workers, falling like a mist around me: *Pedestrian vs. car . . . patient found unresponsive . . . multiple lower extremity deformities . . . open fracture leg . . . ETA ten minutes . . .*

I see Molly's parents' car behind us all the way, running red lights and everything as she sticks like glue to the rear end of the ambulance. When we arrive at the emergency room, I feel as if I'm stuck in space and time, but space and time move at a whirlwind speed, whipping around me. Voices echo and reverberate throughout my body. A thick fog has moved in, and I feel like I'm floating in it, not connected to anything.

Molly helps me field as many questions as possible until Mom comes rushing in. I'm so relieved to see her, my legs literally give way. Mom puts one arm around my shoulders, and I lean against her as she takes over.

Does the patient have insurance? What provider? Is he allergic to any medications? Does he have a history of . . . ?

Molly steers me away from Mom and the hospital staff to

the seating area and sits down next to me. The seating area is about half full. All the people in there look the way I feel, with their faces drawn and tight, eyes bloodshot, tissues wadded up tightly in fists. Some pace with their arms folded across their chests; others sit with their faces in their hands. A few dart in and out of the room, their clothes smelling like the kids from the smoking section at school.

Molly and I sit silently, gripping each other's hands, and watch Mom call Nanaji and Naniji a couple of times to get all the information needed to fill out forms.

There's a TV monitor in the corner of the room with a newsperson updating us on Michael Jordan's divorce, and informing us that Alicia Keys, U2, and India.Arie lead the nominations for the Grammy awards.

Mom reassures Nanaji and Naniji that she will call them as soon as we have more information.

A few moments later a nurse informs Mom that Uncle Sandeep is being taken down the hall for a CT scan of his chest, abdomen, and pelvis. Mom reaches out to hold on to the wall for a moment, as if for support, before returning to the paperwork.

Once all the forms are filled out, she hurries over to us. "Girls! Sammy, are you all right? What happened?"

Having Mom next to me cuts through some of the fog. "I . . . some guys—Chuck and Rick and Simon—started messing with me in the parking lot . . ."

Her eyes widen. "Those same boys from . . ."

I nod. "Second grade."

Her face splotches with color and the muscle at her jaw jumps. She reaches out to stroke my cheek.

"I tried calling you and there was no answer."

She closes her eyes and drops her head back. "I turned off the ringer so that I could be alone with my thoughts for a while. I checked for messages as soon as I could. Why didn't you leave a message?"

"I needed someone right then! I didn't want to leave a message." The last part of my sentence is half sob. I draw in a shaky breath and continue. "I called Uncle Sandeep and—and he came, and when I told him what happened, he got mad and ran out to—to . . . I don't know what, but when I ran back up to the parking lot, I heard their car squeal out and . . ."

Molly strokes my back as the tears drop onto my shirt. I chew on a fingernail to stop the trembling of my chin and lips.

Mom folds me in her arms, and I let her smell wash over me. The tears turn into a stream as my ribs expand and contract with giant sobs.

"Oh, baby . . . my darling . . . ," she croons. Then, in a hard, icy voice, "Something has to be done about those boys."

Molly's still rubbing my back, but I can hear her sniffles next to me. I stay in the cocoon of Mom's arms until the squeak of doctor shoes on linoleum gets closer.

"Mrs. Ahluwahlia?"

Mom keeps one arm around me as she turns to the doctor. "Ms. Ahluwahlia. I'm Sandeep's sister."

The doctor, Dr. Schiff, nods and sits down across from us. "Your brother is in the pre-op holding area. We'll need your consent for surgery. He has bilateral leg fractures, including a femoral fracture as well as open left tibia and fibula fractures. Any objections to a blood transfusion, should it become necessary?"

I slip back into the fog. I feel as if I'm not touching anything, like there's a layer of air keeping me from making actual contact with anything solid around me. My eyes are drawn back to the newscaster. "Earlier this month, Ibn al-Shaykh al-Libi, believed to be a Libyan paramilitary trainer for Al-Qaeda, was captured and interrogated by American and Egyptian forces. The information he provided under intense questioning was cited by the Bush Administration as possible evidence of a connection between Saddam Hussein and Al-Qaeda . . ."

Mom's name is called, and the nurse at the window tells us we are allowed a quick visit with Uncle Sandeep while he's in the pre-op holding area.

When we get there, he's awake and conscious, but not very verbal. There's some bruising on his face and blood caked on his clothes. My lungs are not working properly. I can't seem to get enough air as I float around in the fog. I want one of my uncle's bear hugs. I want him to say something that makes no sense to me so that I can laugh with him. I want him to talk about "the peace." But no matter how hard I try, I can't seem to swim through all the fog. I see his lips moving, but I can't hear him. Someone's arm—Molly's?—is holding me up. I notice that Mom's fingers are paler than ever and tremble as she strokes her brother's hand.

Soon we're sent back to the waiting room as Uncle Sandeep

is wheeled to the operating room for surgery. Mom calls Nanaji and Naniji, and Molly calls her parents.

"Hi, Ma." I can hear the rise and fall of Naniji's voice through Mom's cell phone. "He's going into the OR right now. . . . I don't know, Ma. He looks—he seemed . . ." and then a sob. Mom's fingers stroke her forehead, covering her eyes, but I see the tears dangling from her chin and her shoulders shivering.

I reach out for her hand.

The news guy is saying, "Daniel Pearl, the South Asia bureau chief of the *Wall Street Journal*, was kidnapped by terrorists in Karachi, Pakistan, and is believed to still be alive. . . ."

Mom grips my hand tight and takes a deep breath in. "He's going to be fine, Ma," she says into her cell phone. "He's being well cared for. . . . No, I'm all right. Sammy is here and so is Molly. . . . a good friend of ours . . . yes, I will . . . yes, Ma . . . and . . . thanks . . . okay, bye."

Molly hangs up seconds after Mom. "My mom told me to tell you she and Dad are praying for Uncle Sandeep."

"Tell them thank you," Mom says with a small smile. She puts her cell phone in her bag.

"Thank God he's still . . . ," Molly breathes.

I close my eyes to shut out the newscaster's voice and hold tight to Mom's hand.

Molly's eyes fill as she turns to face Mom. "I thought . . . I thought the worst when I came out and saw him lying there on the ground with Sammy screaming over him."

"Me too," I whisper.

Mom shakes her head and rests her chin in her other hand.

I feel her energy slip away, like it does when she gets lost in moments from the past.

The three of us sit quietly like that for what feels like forever: Mom on my left with her chin perched on one hand, me in the middle, and Molly to my right; all of us gripping one another's hands.

Every now and then, one of us gets up to use the bathroom or to stretch our legs, but none of us wander too far. Mom talks to Nanaji and Naniji twice more before Dr. Schiff arrives.

She sits down in a seat across from Mom. "The surgery is finished, and it went well."

You can almost hear our collective exhale.

The doctor continues. "We washed out the open fractures and stabilized them with external fixators and . . . intramedullary nails . . . left femur nailed . . ."

Molly steps away to answer her phone.

"We're keeping him in the recovery room for a bit; you can see him when he's set up in the hospital room, okay?"

Mom throws her arms around a startled Dr. Schiff. "Thank you."

The doctor smiles. "Not at all. A nurse will come to take you to his room once he's all set up."

As the doctor leaves, Mom dials Nanaji and Naniji's number. She walks away to update them.

"Wow," Molly breathes. Her eyes are like blue swimming pools.

The fog begins to lift. I repeat the doctor's words, "The surgery went well." They feel good, those words.

"Why don't we go to the cafeteria for a bite to eat?" Mom says, coming back from her call. "Molly, thank you for being here and staying. You should probably go on home and get some rest."

Molly looks at me. "You okay, Wally?"

I squeeze her hand. "Better now. Thanks, Moll . . . really."

"My mom said she's bringing over some food tomorrow afternoon for you guys," says Molly, hugging Mom.

Mom nods. "Tell her thank you, again . . . for *everything*."

"Call me tomorrow," Molly says, hugging me good-bye.

Mom and I walk to the cafeteria and get some hot chocolate from one of those machines. We sit down at a table that looks out onto a dark and deserted street corner.

She wraps her hands around the Styrofoam cup. "Your naniji and nanaji were just about hysterical."

The hot chocolate is too hot to drink, so I stir it endlessly with a red plastic straw.

"Still," she continues, "as hysterical as your naniji was, she was something solid for me to cling to. When I'm around her, I become six years old again, in all the bad ways *and* the good."

"I know," I say, finally taking a tiny sip. "Me too . . . with you."

Mom's eyes go soft as she gazes at me. "You are the love of my life, Sammy."

And in that moment, I know it's the truth. I know, in a way I've never known before, how much my mother loves me and has always loved me. And that everything she has done, no matter how much it pissed me off, was because of that truth.

She stares out the window and begins to recount old memories, like pulling out dusty clothes from an old trunk: me and her at the MacFaddens' family get-togethers early on, when we were just getting to know their family; Molly sleeping over for the first time and the two of us jumping on my bed until the frame broke; the trip Mom and I took to the Bahamas when I was seven, and I got stung by a jellyfish. I join in, getting carried along by her lulling current, adding my own version of certain memories and filling in details from my side.

We carefully stay away from anything that might take us into Chuck Banfield, Rick Taylor, and Simon Monroe territory. We're still raw but coming back slowly, pulling each other out; one sip of hot chocolate plus one memory at a time. I realize this is what we've always done, me and Mom, just the two of us. And it'll always be there, this special gift that we've created between ourselves, glowing like a moon and giving us warmth when we need it.

After a while, Mom looks at her watch. "Let's go see if they've taken Sandeep up to a room yet."

We get up and walk back to the waiting room. The fog is almost all gone. A lightness fills me.

A nurse tells us Uncle Sandeep is in a room and directs us to the floor and wing. The walk to see him is a silent one. The whiteness of the rooms we pass on the way there is jarring.

As if reading my mind, Mom murmurs, "We need to get some flowers. Why didn't we think of that?"

We stop just outside the door to Uncle Sandeep's room. There is an empty bed closest to us, and Uncle Sandeep is behind a half-drawn curtain on the bed next to the window. We can't see his face from where we're standing.

Seeing him lying in the parking lot scared the hell out of me. I seriously thought he was dead. I couldn't breathe for a long moment, then when I did, all I could do was scream.

Mom lingers a moment just inside the doorway before striding in. "What—flying off the roof with an umbrella wasn't enough for you, Sandeep?"

I walk in more cautiously. When his face comes into view, I see that he's grimacing as Mom leans over to kiss his forehead.

"Looks worse than it is," he says. His words slur into one another, like he's speaking through a mouthful of cotton, and he takes occasional pauses for air. "But look on the bright side. I'm drugged up, legally, and am the sole focus of two of my favorite women in the world."

Relief floods through me. *He's still alive! He's trying to crack jokes!* I grab onto the side of the bed to keep from throwing my arms around him. Tears slide out of the corners of my eyes and down my face.

Mom's eyes glisten too. "To quote Papa: You are a damn fool, Sandeep."

His turban is sitting on the table next to the bed, still wrapped up, looking like an upside-down forest green boat with a trail of fabric swirling out behind it. I notice that the few grays straggling through his topknot match the ones in his mustache and beard. He looks different without his turban— older, smaller. It's like his crown. It expands him and makes him as big as he is on the inside.

Uncle Sandeep's grin fades as he turns to me. "Samar, are you okay? Those boys, they didn't . . . ?"

I dab my face with a sleeve and lean across Mom to kiss him on the forehead like she did. It's hard to talk through all the stuff in my chest. I struggle to form words. "I'm okay, Uncle Sandeep. They gave me a scare, but I got away before anything happened. That's what I was trying to tell you when you took off."

Mom heaves an exaggerated sigh. "That's exactly what he did when he jumped off the roof—charged ahead without getting all the information."

"I wanted only to have a few words with those boys. Those types of boys only bother people who are at a disadvantage; those who cannot defend themselves, or are not as strong as they are." He stops for a moment to catch his breath, his face full of determination to go on. "When forced to face someone their own size, they turn into frightened little children."

"I agree," Mom says, "but those boys were drunk. They were in an altered state of mind, Sandeep."

"Precisely. Which is why . . . they could have really harmed Samar."

"Or you," Mom says quietly.

He drops his head back and closes his eyes. "They needed to know, Sharan . . . they would be held accountable."

"There are better ways to do that," Mom says firmly.

I wish she would stop. "Mom, can't we talk about this another time?"

Uncle Sandeep looks off at a point on the ceiling for a

moment. "She's right, Samar," he concedes. "I may have . . . let my emotions get . . . the better of me."

Mom throws an arm in the air. "*May* have?"

I shoot her a look, but Uncle Sandeep gives her what passes for a lopsided grin. "Okay, fine, Sharan, you've made your point. You were right . . . again. Happy now?"

Mom tries to look smug, but her eyelashes are wet and she doesn't quite pull it off. "Yes, I am, actually," she says gently.

"God," I say, shaking my head. "I can totally see you guys as kids."

We stay until he drifts off to sleep, neither of us wanting to leave. Eventually one of the nurses comes in to tell us what the official hospital visiting hours are and sends us on our way.

On the way out, Mom stops to pick up more hot chocolate for us from the hospital cafeteria.

When we walk out into the parking lot, the sky is just beginning to glow indigo as the sun begins its climb up over the horizon.

"Been a long time since I've seen the sun come up like that," Mom says, squinting into the sky. "It's something, isn't it? Like a symphony, with the sun as the conductor—there he is, leading the whole thing, pointing at each color to wake up and perform its magic."

We watch the colors change for several moments as day emerges from night, like stepping into a fresh new beginning. We let the sun's rays seep deep into our skin and send them back out in our own way to write a new story on a new page. All of a sudden, it occurs to me that every day we get this chance. Every day, we can decide which way to take the moments that make up our lives, like being in a car and steering in the direction you want to go.

Mom holds my hand the whole ride back to our house, but we sit in silence with our own thoughts. When we walk in the door, I'm relieved to be back home in our little house. It wraps around me like one of Mom's hugs, with all her smells and loving words. Without warning, all the events of last night, last month, and all the months since Uncle Sandeep showed up on our doorstep catch up with me.

I take off my boots, coat, and gloves, and walk to the kitchen table as the sobs slash through to my core. Mom slides a chair next to me, and holds me tight for as long as I need it.

When we finally crawl into our beds, the sun is climbing high into the sky. *What a gorgeous day it's going to be,* I think, as the sounds of the world coming alive outside my window begin to fade far into the distance.

Then I have one of the most vivid dreams I've ever had. I'm on a boat. A biting wind howls around us, but the sun shines, bright and fierce. The boat sways on the surface of the peacock blue waters off the Jersey shore. Nanaji stands stoically to one side of me, and Naniji leans against Mom on my other side. Molly's not touching me, but I can feel her behind me.

I hold up an urn and tilt it to let some ashes fly. They pour out and spread, sitting in the air like a twinkling mist. Little jewels in the bright afternoon sun, going up and out and down and everywhere. The ashes cling to my skin like talcum powder.

When I try to brush them off, they only grind finer, sinking under the surface to burrow deep inside.

Sun dust.

A breeze whispers faintly into my ear, *Shine, little* muni, *shine.*

I close my eyes and turn my face to the beaming warmth of the sun, realizing that the ashes in the urn are mine.

I wake up in a cold sweat and breathe deeply to calm myself before falling back asleep.

When I wake up again, I ask Mom about it. Her eyes light up. She says it might mean that I'm letting a part of myself go, but the most radiant parts of what I'm letting go are staying with me, clinging to me and being deeply absorbed. What I don't need is flying away into the dust.

Chapter 20

Warm weather does wonders for my mood. Now that it's summer and the birds are having little hangouts in our backyard and Mom's garden is in full bloom, it's a lot easier to look back at the past few months.

Word got around quick about what happened in the parking lot. Maybe that was the reason my teachers took it easier on me, or maybe my performance-under-pressure mechanism kicked in. I don't know, but somehow I made it through to graduation.

Rick Taylor, Chuck Banfield, and Simon Monroe were all expelled from school and charged with assault, driving while impaired, hit-and-run, and a bunch of other charges Mom rattled off to me. Because the boys were all over eighteen, they were tried as adults in court.

The principal made several announcements in school about underage drinking and driving while impaired, as well as restating several times the school's zero-tolerance policy on racial and sexual harassment. All future school dances were canceled until further notice.

The first school year after the Trade Center attacks, America moved on: shopping, working, loving, growing— almost back to usual. But something fundamental had changed, deep inside the nation, and the world. Deep inside me and everyone I knew. Nothing would ever be the same. Something had died, and we needed to spill the ashes to allow the most dazzling specks to come back and burrow themselves under our skin.

A couple of months after the dance, I heard from Molly, who heard from Bobbi, who got it from one of her numerous "sources," that Mike was dating a blond junior on the cheerleading squad named Brittany. Bobbi, being Bobbi, was "helpful" enough to point Brittany out to me in the halls.

Whenever she passed me, Brittany threw nervous, jittery looks my way. But my attention was so focused on other areas of my life, like college, meeting new members of my family, and learning more about myself and my mom and our history, that my relationship with Mike already felt like something far, far away.

Uncle Sandeep stayed in the hospital for about ten days, recovering and undergoing physical therapy. He had another surgery after that first one and brags to anyone who'll listen that he has plates and screws and pins in his bones.

He still gives me regular lectures on the importance of learning more about myself. "You know what the ancient Egyptians used to say? 'Know thyself.' That's the secret door to everything, Samar—*know* thyself."

The more I know myself, *really* know myself, he says, the

more I'll see that there's actually no difference between me and everyone else. "We're not humans on a spiritual journey, Samar," he always says, wagging a finger at me. "We are spirits on a human journey. Remember that."

Yeah, okay, Uncle Sandeep.

And Mom. Reconnecting with her family has changed something deep inside her. It's obvious to everyone—even Molly mentioned it. She's softer, somehow, in ways I can't quite put my finger on. She now volunteers at the new Center for Young People downtown, as a specialist in the issues of immigrant youth. She seems more alive than ever, after she comes home from working with young women struggling with things similar to what she struggled with when she lived at home with Nanaji and Naniji.

One quiet spring evening, Mom and I were having tea together at the kitchen table. All of a sudden, she looked at a point somewhere in the space between us, as if focusing on another scene, in another time.

"My father once told me," she said, "that without knowing ourselves, our history, we are all light feathers, torn from the body of a free bird and drifting alone in the wind."

I sat quietly and waited, knowing that she was sort of here and sort of somewhere else.

"My grandmother had five girls," she began, "and she loved them deeply. One of them is your naniji. The three eldest went to Fiji with their parents, and my mother and her younger sister were brought up in Punjab, by an aunt and uncle who had spent the majority of their lives in Britain . . . ," and she continued until three a.m.

My heart raced as I listened to her story. *My* story. It's a saga that I'm a part of. A huge line that goes way back into a distant, far-off past. All these layers and points on a time line. Gone, but not forgotten . . . a long-held memory whispered from the lips of the past into the ear of the future.

One other thing I've learned through Uncle Sandeep and Mom's conversations—because as much as they sometimes like to bicker, they really are very similar. I see that we're all, each and every one of us, like little palaces with invaluable, one-of-a-kind treasures inside. And if there's a part of ourselves that we don't claim, whether we forget to, choose not to, or feel forced to, we put that unique, precious piece outside on the porch. And we let the world know we don't want it, it's not welcome inside. Then the world is free to treat that precious valuable in whatever way it wants. But it's still a part of us, even though we've closed the door. And at some point we have to come back outside to get it, in whatever shape it's in.

I know now that, in a way, Mom was the treasure Uncle Sandeep came back to get that Saturday morning. The forgotten cast-off on the porch. Her silent screams rang out loud and clear in those photographs in the family albums, if anyone had chosen to take notice. I never would have thought so at first, since she was the one who cut off ties, but to be ninety minutes away, living in the same state, with no contact for fifteen years, is a two-way street. For years they let her stay there, just outside the door.

So Uncle Sandeep brought her, and me, back inside. Strangely enough, that's when I brought them back inside too. "Them" being Naniji, Nanaji, Uncle Sandeep, my heritage, history, and everything else that brought me here, to this moment.

I now have two bona fide South Asian friends, Shazia and Balvir—my "peeps." I also am a regular poster on South Asian forums and have an entire cyber-community of former and recovering coconuts. I tell all of them that coconuts are very resilient and often grow taller than many of the plants around them, usually in less than optimal conditions.

Ever since the night of the Midwinter Dance, Mom and Uncle Sandeep have stuck to a regular weekend schedule of hanging out. Every Sunday they get together for brunch and drop me off to hang out with Nanaji and Naniji. Some days Mom comes in when she comes to pick me up and stays for a bit before we head home.

Even though she won't admit it, I saw the look of relief on Mom's face when Naniji and Nanaji decided not to sell the house for a little longer. As Nanaji said, "You never know—your uncle could still get married, and then we'll wish we had all this space again for the grandchildren."

Things aren't as warm and fuzzy as I'd like them to be with Mom and her parents, but she's trying. And that's something. Uncle Sandeep says, "It's progress, Samar. Delhi wasn't built in a day. Brick by brick. Give them time."

So that's where I am this Sunday: in Nanaji and Naniji's kitchen with the sun spilling liquid gold onto the countertops.

"*Grind* them, *beta*, don't pound."

I turn my attention back to the task at hand. Naniji throws a few more cloves into the marble mortar and pestle set and wraps her warm marshmallow hand around my fingers to show me how it's done. "*Han*, like that . . . see? Perfect!"

I peer into the combination of spices in the marble bowl. "Okay, so we've got cardamom, cloves, fennel . . . and what was that last one?"

"I don't know in English, but in Punjabi, we call it *ajwain*," she says, tucking a small corner of her *chunni* scarf into her mouth and measuring out teaspoons of sugar. She dumps the sugar into a separate small steel bowl and mixes some crushed cinnamon in with it.

When I've finished grinding the spices, Naniji pours the mixture into a pot of boiling water. Next she stirs in the sugar-cinnamon mixture.

Nanaji sits on a stool at their kitchen island, reading the weekly newspaper, *Times of Punjab*. He glances at us over his reading glasses and says a few words to Naniji in Punjabi. She nods.

"Samar, *beta*, come here," he calls.

Naniji nods to me. "Go on, we must allow the chai to simmer now. We want to give the flavors a chance to mingle, *nah*? I'll heat up the pakoras in the meantime."

Nanaji puts his paper down and beckons for me to follow. Before I even get close, he heads toward the back of the house. I follow, wondering what he plans to share with me today. Each time I've visited, Nanaji has shared something new about himself or his life.

During my last visit, he showed me old, sepia-stained photos of when he was in the military in India. The time before that, he took out a beautiful, hand-carved, wooden and ivory box that was his mother's. Nanaji pressed it into my hands and told me to take good care of it. As the first grandchild, it was now rightfully mine.

I've placed it in my trunk, next to my Winnie the Pooh stars and moon yum-yum. When I showed the box to Mom, she stared at it in stunned silence, fingering the intricate carvings gingerly as tears welled up in her eyes.

Today I follow Nanaji out into the sunroom that faces their huge backyard. "Come here," he says. I stand next to him and look at the plants all around us. Some are as tall as I am, growing out of clay pots on the floor, others are on benches that come to my waist. "These are the plants," he says, pointing to all of the plants.

I nod. "They look great, Nanaji."

He shakes his head. "Samar, look closely at these plants. What do you see? What do you smell?"

I furrow my brow. I lean closer to a bushy one with dark green leaves. I don't see anything unusual. Again he shakes his head. He snaps a leaf off and hands it to me. "Smell," he commands.

Before the leaf even reaches my nose, I'm bombarded with its scent. "Cardamom!" I breathe.

He looks pleased. "Absolutely," he says, walking away. "I wanted you to see the source of those seeds and barks you are grinding up with your naniji." Then, in a quieter, almost reverent voice, he says,

"I planted every single one of these herbs and spices. These hands nurtured them from tiny seeds wrapped in paper."

Nanaji shows me a few more of his plants: curry leaves, fennel, anise, cinnamon. He walks with his hands behind his rigid back, his voice booming but gentle.

When we're done, he puts a hand on my shoulder—the closest he ever comes to hugging me. "*Bas*. Come, let us have chai with your naniji."

We walk back to the kitchen, where Naniji has already poured the chai into huge mugs. There is a plate of pakoras and a plate of sweets on the table as well. "Samar, you must always have something sweet and something savory to serve your guests," she says, putting a small plate in front of me and piling it high with the snacks. "And pakoras are easy to make. We don't have much time left today, but next time I will show you how to make them. These sweets were your mother's favorite when she was a girl." She pulls out a red box with a gold bow and places it next to my plate. "There are more in here—take them for Sharanjit when you go."

My heart feels buoyant, like a feather attached to a free bird, soaring high into the clouds. This is a feeling I've been getting a lot lately. I stare into my chai, eyes welling up. "I wish I had this before," I say softly. "Like, when I was growing up . . ."

Naniji laughs and puts a hand on the top of my head. "So is it all over, then? You're done growing up?" She crinkles her eyes and looks at me the same way that Mom does. "We have a lot of time to make up. All is not lost, *beta*."

I know she's right. I should do what Mom always says and

"savor the present." I raise the cup of chai to my lips and, in spite of my trembling chin, sip a tiny amount of the creamy, sweet concoction. I think about how, in the relatively short amount of time since Uncle Sandeep rang our doorbell, he taught this coconut to shine like the moon.

Right now, the summer stretches out before me like a wide, sparkling, silver sheet of ocean. At the end of summer, Sarah Lawrence College awaits. It was one of my choices when Molly and I were sending our applications out. NYU was, of course, my first pick because it was where Molly and I talked about being roommates together. That was when I so desperately wanted to be part of her extended family.

But when I was looking at my acceptance letters and deciding where I truly wanted to go, one tagline stood out: *You are different. So are we.* On their website, they had a quote from one of the founders of the school: "Trying to define yourself is like trying to bite your own teeth."

These days, in spite of Mom's insistence all my life that I'm no different from anyone else, I'm kind of happy with my differences. I've decided it's not such a bad thing after all to have a few of those.

It was like the folks at Sarah Lawrence were speaking directly to me and everything I'd gone through in the last six months. I scoured their website and fell in love with the sociology curriculum: "Students investigate the ways in which social structures and institutions affect individual experience and shape competing definitions of social situations, issues, and identities."

I thought about Balvir's definition of a coconut: brown on the outside, white on the inside, mixed-up, confused. And then Uncle Sandeep's: *The coconut is also a symbol of resilience, Samar. Even in conditions where there's very little nourishment and even less nurturance, it flourishes, growing taller than most of the plants around it.*

Talk about competing definitions. That settled it for me. I want to investigate what's made the experiences of four Sikh Indian women living in America—Mom, Balvir, me, and Naniji—so vastly different, when we all spring from the same resilient coconut tree.

Molly will be going to the Fashion Institute of Technology in New York City in the fall. She's so delighted that she's jumping and popping like mustard seeds in Naniji's frying pan. It's contagious; you can't help but jump and pop with her in her excitement.

I look at the soft grooves around Naniji's eyes. She reaches up to tighten the silvery white bun on her head. When she looks at me again, I see Mom's eyes the way they might be in another twenty years or so. And quite possibly my own, another twenty or thirty years after that.

Naniji wraps a hand around one of mine and smiles. "Tell us again, *beta.*"

I take another sip of my tea and begin to tell my grandparents, again, the story about the day I came home and found Uncle Sandeep at our front door. "There was a man wearing a turban ringing our doorbell. . . ."

Did you love this book?

Want to get access to
the hottest books for free?

Log on to simonandschuster.com/pulseit

to find out how to join,

get access to cool sweepstakes,

and hear about your favorite authors!

Become part of Pulse IT and tell us what you think!

  SIMON & SCHUSTER BFYR

Margaret K.
McElderry Books

SIMON
PULSE

POWERFUL

BOOKS ABOUT STRONG YOUNG WOMEN

HUSH: AN IRISH PRINCESS' TALE
by Donna Jo Napoli

OUTSIDE BEAUTY
by Cynthia Kadohata

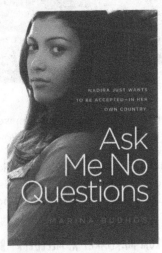

ASK ME NO QUESTIONS
by Marina Budhos

THE REMINDER
by Rune Michaels

From ATHENEUM BOOKS *for* YOUNG READERS
Published by SIMON & SCHUSTER

SAGE WANTS NOTHING MORE THAN TO BE LIKE MONA,
THE MOST POPULAR GIRL IN SCHOOL—
SO SHE DECIDES TO *BE* MONA.

BUT CAN SAGE SUCCEED?
AND AT WHAT COST?

"Teens . . . will recognize themselves
in these pages."—*Kirkus Reviews*

"Easton handles difficult issues such as popularity,
a bipolar parent, poverty, and weight in a sensitive
and frequently comical fashion."—*Booklist*

FROM MARGARET K. McELDERRY BOOKS
PUBLISHED BY SIMON & SCHUSTER

TEEN.SimonandSchuster.com

Sometimes all you have to go on is blind faith.

WINNER OF THE 2009 GREEN EARTH BOOK AWARD FOR YOUNG ADULT FICTION

Fourteen-year-old Zoe wonders how she'll survive when her mother decides to move from the northwest coast to the midwest—leaving Zoe's father behind.

Miserable and away from the ocean she loves, Zoe loses her bearings completely. A shoplifting episode lands her in a work program at a local nature preserve, amidst what look to her like endless weeds. But the work there starts to stabilize Zoe, and when she meets a boy who shares her love of wild things, it seems she might be home after all. Until a disastrous fire threatens everything she has come to care about . . .

From Margaret K. McElderry Books · Published by Simon & Schuster · TEEN.SimonandSchuster.com

Heartfelt novels from award-winning author D. Anne Love

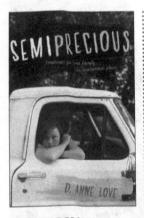

SEMIPRECIOUS

"In D. Anne Love's *Semiprecious*, Garnet Hubbard speaks in a voice so strong and true I could have listened to her forever."

—FRANCES O'ROARK DOWELL, author of *Where I'd Like to Be*, *The Secret Language of Girls*, *Dovey Coe*, and *Chicken Boy*

DEFYING THE DIVA

"Skillfully captures the painful reality of teen bullying while also telling Haley's humorous and sincere story of growing up."

—*KIRKUS REVIEWS*

PICTURE PERFECT

"Genuine. Both uplifting and realistic, making its impact all the more powerful."

—*PUBLISHERS WEEKLY*

"A rewarding read."

—*KIRKUS REVIEWS*

From Margaret K. McElderry Books
Published by Simon & Schuster

TEEN.SIMONANDSCHUSTER.COM